# The Trouble with Portals

## Adventures in Reason

Kris Langman

Post Hoc Publishing

The Trouble with Portals
Logic to the Rescue 2

Print Edition
Post Hoc Publishing

# Chapter One

## A Visitor

NIKKI MURROW WAS sitting in the bleachers of her high school gymnasium when she heard a voice coming from under her feet.

"Miss! I think I need a pair of them shiny purple pants."

Nikki gasped and jumped up, spilling her Coke onto the neck of the person sitting in front of her.

"Blast it!" yelled Tina, the captain of the school's debate team. "You've ruined my new silk top!"

"I'm sorry, Tina," said Nikki. "I'll pay for your top." Nikki sat back down, wiping her sticky hands on her Westlake Debate Team t-shirt. She must have imagined the voice whispering about shiny purple pants. She sat still and tried to listen. The gym was noisy with students shouting and basketballs pounding as the Westlake team warmed up for the first game of the season. The voice must have been a student sitting nearby, talking about the team uniforms. They were shiny and purple, with yellow trim.

"Miss! I need some shoes also. Mr. Fuzz got me some nice new leather boots out of a Castle Cogent storage room, but I can see lots of shoes from down here and ain't nobody wearing boots like mine. I stick out like a mule at a fancy-dress ball, and I need to blend in and be all sneaky-like."

Nikki stuck her head between her knees and peered under the bleachers. A small blond head was just barely visible in the shadows, poking out from behind a pile of gymnastic mats. A scrawny little hand with very dirty fingernails waved at her.

"Curio!" Nikki hissed. "What are you doing here!?"

"Well, Miss," Curio began.

"Sssshhhh!" hissed Nikki. "Stay there. I'm coming down." She slid past the students on her row of the bleachers and scrambled down the metal supports to the floor of the gym. The game had started and all eyes were on the two teams as they went for the tip-up. Nikki darted under the bleachers and threaded her way through piles of lacrosse sticks, deflated basketballs, crushed soda cans, and smelly gym shoes. Curio's blond head glowed dimly in the semi-darkness.

"Hello, Miss," said Curio, giving her a cheerful, gap-toothed grin. "It's nice to . . ."

"Not here," said Nikki. "Follow me."

She led Curio out from under the bleachers to a side door of the gym. They slipped through unnoticed and emerged into an empty hallway lined with lockers and a scuffed linoleum floor. A faulty fluorescent light flickered on and off as Nikki opened the door to a janitor's closet and pulled Curio inside. She shut the door firmly and yanked on a chain to turn on the overhead light.

Curio glanced around. "Miss, this is the portal entrance. I came through here two days ago."

Nikki nodded and continued past him to the dark depths of the closet where an old boiler sat quietly rusting. It had been replaced by a new electrical heating system years ago. She opened the boiler's coal door and peered inside. She half expected to see the alley in the Realm of Reason where this portal had led her a year ago, but there was nothing inside except for cobwebs and a faint smell of coal dust. She closed the coal door and stood looking down at Curio, her arms crossed.

Curio shrugged. "Sometimes the portal's there and sometimes it ain't." He hitched up the baggy pair of woolen trousers he was wearing. "About them purple pants, Miss. Do you think you can get me some? These wool ones are making me scratch something awful. And maybe a shiny purple shirt also? I noticed nobody here is wearing a linen shirt like mine."

Nikki waved an impatient hand. "We can go to Goodwill and I'll buy you jeans and a T-shirt. I have some allowance money. In the meantime don't worry about it. You look a bit like an Amish kid in those clothes. This is Wisconsin. We have a few Amish communities. People aren't going to stare at you."

Curio nodded. "Well, that's good, Miss. Like I said, I want to kinda blend in with the locals. But I really like the look of them purple pants."

"Only basketball players wear those," said Nikki. "And you're too young to be on the team. Now, forget about the purple pants and tell me why you're here."

Curio's normally cheerful expression disappeared from his thin face. "I hates to have to be the one to tell you this, Miss, but you has a visitor. A very unwelcome one."

The skin on the back of Nikki's neck prickled. "I thought I'd imagined it."

Curio's blue eyes looked up at her intently. "So, you saw him?"

Nikki nodded. "I've spent the last three weeks trying to convince myself I'd imagined it. But yes, I saw him. He came through the portal right before me. I caught a glimpse of his black tunic and his sandals before he went through that door." She pointed at the closed door of the closet.

Curio turned and looked at the door. "So, he's somewhere in your place of learning?"

"It's called a high school," said Nikki. "And no, I don't think he's still in the school. Fall term started right after I got back from the

Realm of Reason, and I haven't seen him anywhere."

Curio ran his dirty hands through his hair, making it look even more like a messy blond haystack. "We gots to find him, Miss. We gots to get him back to the Realm. Miss Athena and Mr. Fuzz are awfully upset that such a dangerous character has gone through the portal to your land. No telling what harm he could do here. I think they feel responsible."

Nikki frowned. "Then why didn't Fuzz and Athena come here themselves? They had no trouble getting here a year ago. It seems pretty irresponsible of them to send a little kid like you to follow such a dangerous person as Rufius."

"It weren't like that, Miss," said Curio. "They've been really busy. They gots their hands full trying to train Mr. Bertie to be King. He's not really taking to the job like a fish to water. More like a chicken caught in a waterwheel. So they ordered me to camp out in the alley in Cogent Town and watch for the portal to open again. See, we found out that Rufius had gone in right before you did. A little girl about six years old was playing in the alley, and she told her mother that she'd seen a man in a black tunic walk through the wall. That's how she put it. Anyway, her mother didn't know nothing about the portal, but she thought it was an odd story, so she reported it to a guard on duty at Castle Cogent, and the guard reported it to Mr. Bertie. I mean, to the King. I still has a hard time remembering that Mr. Bertie is now His Majesty. It doesn't help that Mr. Bertie keeps forgetting to wear his crown. He says it gives him a headache."

"So, you just happened to be in the alley when the portal opened again," said Nikki. "And you went through. Pretty risky. Why didn't you just report to Fuzz and Athena that the portal was open again?"

"Well, I had to take my chance, Miss," said Curio. "Don't know how the portal works in your land, but in the Realm we don't have much understanding of its workings. Only a few people know about it at all. Miss Athena and Mr. Fuzz know the most about it. They've been through it the most, but even they don't know how to control it. I figured that if I ran all the way up to the castle and reported that the portal was open again, by the time we got back down to the alley it would be closed."

Nikki nodded, looking down at Curio with a mixture of affection and worry. They'd had a kind of big sister, little brother relationship during her year in the Realm of Reason. She'd always felt responsible for him, and right now she wasn't sure exactly what to do with him. She could try bringing him home with her, though she had no idea how she'd explain him to her mother. Or she could wait in the janitor's closet with him until the portal opened again, which would be hard to explain to the janitor.

Curio, who'd always been oddly perceptive for such a young boy, gave her a pat on the arm. "Don't worry about me, Miss. I've been here two days already with no problems. I've been sleeping on those comfy mats where you found me just now, and I've been getting plenty of food. There's a big room in this here place of learning that has piles of food. I found some chicken last night in a big box which was really cold. It was very strange, as I didn't see no ice anywhere inside it."

"It's called a refrigerator," said Nikki. "It's how we keep food from spoiling. And the room you found was the school's cafeteria. It's where all the students eat lunch. Well, where most of the students eat lunch. I usually take a sack lunch out to a bench by the soccer field. When I eat in the cafeteria Tina and her gang throw French fries at my head. They still haven't forgiven me for making our debate team lose the state championship."

Curio's pale little face hardened. "I dunno what French fries are, or who this Tina is, but she sounds like a mean little bully. We gots plenty of them in the Realm. When I was working for my master one of the other servants used to grab my neck and dunk my head in the slop trough out in the pig pen. The pigs didn't appreciate it and neither did I. Want me to have some words with this Tina person?"

"No," said Nikki. "I can handle her. We've got bigger problems, like how to get you home again."

"Well, Miss," said Curio, "it seems to me that I should stay here a while. I needs to track down Rufius. Find out where he went and then report it to Mr. Fuzz and Miss Athena."

Nikki was shaking her head before he finished. "That seems way too dangerous. We should wait until the portal opens again and send you back through. If Fuzz and Athena want Rufius returned to the Realm they can send castle guards through the portal to hunt him down."

"I'm not gonna arrest Rufius on my own, Miss," said Curio. "I may be only ten going on eleven, but I ain't stupid. I'm only gonna find out where he is. And besides, despite being a nasty piece of slime, he ain't really that dangerous when it comes to fighting and stuff. I ain't never seen him actually attack anybody. He always gets other people to do his dirty work for him." He sat down on an overturned bucket and began untying his leather boots. "Pardon me bare feet, Miss," he said. "But my toes is cramping something awful."

"What's that?" asked Nikki. Curio's right foot had a leather strap around it.

"It's supposed to hold me toes on," said Curio, digging his hand into one of his boots and pulling out a little woolen bag which was dribbling flax seeds. "I strap this here bag to my foot and it helps with my balance. The royal shoemaker up at Castle Cogent made it for me. Before I got it I kept lurching sideways. Turns out that losing two toes makes you walk like the town drunk."

Nikki stared down at Curio's tiny foot with its two missing toes and wanted to cry. He'd lost them in their fight against Rufius, when Rufius led a violent revolt to take over the Realm of Reason. Curio's foot was bleeding where the leather strap cut into it. That decided it, Nikki thought to herself. Curio would have to come home with her.

Her mother could take Curio to a doctor and get him a proper prosthetic for his injured foot. She just had to come up with a good story. Maybe she could say Curio was fleeing an abusive home. That wasn't too far from the truth. Curio was an orphan, a pedestal baby as they called it in the Realm of Reason. Abandoned or orphaned children were left on a stone pedestal in the middle of the town square.

"Put your boots back on," said Nikki. "You're coming home with me."

"Gosh, Miss," said Curio. "Really? That's awful nice of you. Do you live with a master? I hope he treats you good."

"I live with my mother," said Nikki. "My Dad, well, he's not around. And we don't have masters here. Actually, it's kind of an offensive word. So I wouldn't mention it if I were you."

"But Miss," said Curio. "If you don't have masters then where do all the pedestal babies go?"

"We don't have those either," said Nikki. "We call them orphans, and usually someone adopts them. They go to live with a new family."

Curio's blue eyes opened wide. "A new family?"

Nikki felt her stomach twist at the longing in Curio's voice. She gave the little boy a quick hug. "Come on. Let's go home. Do you have any belongings?"

"No, Miss," said Curio. "I was so worried that the portal would close before I got through that I just jumped in. Daisy was with me in the alley, and I had a few things in her saddlebags, but I wasn't gonna try bringing a donkey through the portal."

"Okay," said Nikki. "Well let's go get this over with. The hardest part is going to be preventing my mother from calling a social worker. They're people who help children in trouble, and calling them is what most people would do. We need to come up with a good story for why you should stay with me and my mom."

"We don't need no story, Miss," said Curio as he laced up his boots. "I'll just go full pedestal baby." He opened his blue eyes wide, tears began to pour down his cheeks, and he took in big, panicked gulps of air. "Please don't send me away ma'am. Nikki here is me only friend in the whole world. I can't be parted from her. I'll just die if you send me away." He stood up and flashed a mischievous grin. "You can get away with a lot when you go full pedestal baby. Course, it helps if you're small. The bigger kids usually give up on the pedestal baby act and just start stealing food, or coins, or whatever they can get their hands on. Can't say as I blame them. After all, you gotta eat."

Nikki pulled the overhead chain to turn off the light and slowly opened the closet door. No one was in the hallway. She and Curio left the high school and walked quickly through the darkening streets of Madison, Wisconsin. Nikki and her mom lived in the city center, near Lake Monona. It was early evening on a Sunday and the streets were quiet.

Curio stared open-mouthed at the streetlights and the parked cars and the neon signs above shop windows, but he didn't ask any questions until a motorcycle suddenly zoomed around a corner and roared past them. He plastered himself against the front window of a bookshop, shaking from head to toe. "Miss, what . . . I don't understand. Was it a monster?"

"No," said Nikki. "It was just a motorcycle. And these are just cars." She pointed at a Honda Civic parked in front of them. "They're ways of moving from place to place, just like the wagons and carts in the Realm of Reason. The only difference is that cars go a lot faster than wagons. You'll get used to them. But in the meantime watch out when you're walking around. Cars don't always stop for pedestrians and you can get badly hurt if one hits you."

Curio looked like he would prefer to remain plastered to the shop window permanently, but Nikki gently peeled him off and kept her arm around his shoulders for the remaining few blocks.

"Here we are," said Nikki, stopping in front of a small red-brick apartment building. It had a neatly mown patch of lawn and carefully trimmed hedges surrounding three yellow rose bushes. Swags of ivy hung down the walls of the building, swaying gently in the evening breeze. "My mom and I live on the top floor. Old Mrs. Evanston has the ground floor, and the middle floor is empty right now."

"It's a very nice house, Miss," Curio said, his voice shaking a bit. "Them candles," he said, pointing at the light showing through the lace curtains on the ground floor. "How do you get them so bright? I saw even brighter ones at your place of learning, but I couldn't figure out where the wax was."

"They're not candles," said Nikki, unlocking the lobby door. "I'll explain later. Right now we need to focus on convincing my mother to let you stay here." She silently wondered how on earth she was going to explain modern-day Madison to someone who'd lived all his life in the Realm of Reason, a land at least five-hundred years behind her world in terms of technology. And she wondered how much she *should* explain. If she sent Curio back to the Realm of Reason with his head full of facts about modern technology it could have serious consequences for the Realm. She'd be meddling in its normal pace of development, possibly introducing technological ideas it wasn't ready for. It was a problem she'd wrestled with during her entire year in the Realm.

An explosion of barking interrupted her thoughts.

"That sounds like one of Castle Cogent's guard dogs," said Curio, edging away from the door where the barking was coming from. "Is it dangerous?"

"No," said Nikki. "It's just Mrs. Evanston's malti-poo. He's a little fluff ball that only weighs about five pounds. But he thinks he's a German shepherd." She led the way up an elegant staircase with a carved walnut banister. The apartment building was showing its age, but when it had been built in the 1920's it had been a showcase of design, with walnut paneling and mosaics on each landing depicting scenes of frolicking Greek gods. Some of the mosaic pieces had fallen off over the years. Mars, the god of war, was missing both arms. The Aphrodite on the ceiling was headless and the water nymphs surrounding her looked like they had a skin rash. Nikki was used to the decay and didn't give the moldy scenes a second glance. Curio, on the other hand, stared at them as if they were going to come to life and pelt him with their missing limbs.

"Is this place haunted, Miss?" he asked, scooting past the headless Aphrodite.

"No," laughed Nikki. "And since when do you believe in ghosts? You have more sense than that. The building's just a bit gloomy, what with all the dark wooden paneling. Come on. I live on the top floor. There's no mosaics up there, so it's more cheerful."

When they reached the third floor landing a door squeaked open and a tall, thin woman with long dark hair appeared. She wore jeans and a gauzy flowered top. Other than the grey streaks in her hair she closely resembled Nikki.

"I was wondering who was coming up the stairs," she said. "I didn't expect you back for hours. Surely the game's not over yet."

"No," said Nikki. "I just had a stomach ache so I left early." She put an arm around Curio's shoulders. "Mom, this is Curio. He's been having trouble at home. A lot of trouble. And he needs a place to stay. Can he stay with us for a while?"

A startled expression passed across Mrs. Murrow's face but was quickly suppressed. She gave Curio a warm smile and took him by the hand. "Why don't we go inside and talk about it?" She led them into the apartment and shut the front door. "Nikki, take your friend into the living room while I make some hot chocolate. And clear those American Chemical Society journals off the sofa so we have room to sit down. Put them on the desk in my office."

"Do you have to use the toilet?" Nikki asked, opening the bathroom door.

Curio poked his head in and gasped. "Miss, what are all these white sculptures? And why is the light so bright?"

"They're not sculptures," said Nikki. "It's just a porcelain tub and a sink and toilet. You know, for washing yourself and for doing, um, the necessary."

Curio's ears turned red. "Oh," he said. "Gosh, Miss. I couldn't do that in here. It's too clean and fancy. I'll just go outside and find a handy bush. That's what I been doing at your place of learning."

"Don't be silly," said Nikki. "If you're going to stay here for a while you'll have to get used to using a toilet. It's not that different from using the outhouses in the Realm of Reason. You sit on the seat, and when you're done you push on this metal handle. Then you wash your hands in the sink." She turned on the cold-water tap, soaped up her hands with a bar of Dial soap, rinsed, and turned off the water.

Curio watched her every move, fascinated. He tried turning the water tap on and off, on and off, until Nikki gently pried his hand off it.

"Where does the water come from, Miss?" he asked.

Nikki shook her head. "It's complicated and I'm not getting into all that right now. Put on your best pedestal-baby face and let's go talk to my mother."

Mrs. Murrow was setting a tray with three mugs of hot chocolate on the coffee table in the living room. Nikki took one and sat down on the lumpy sofa which was covered with a threadbare blanket of dubious Navajo heritage. Curio sat down next to her.

Mrs. Murrow handed him a mug and sat in a leather arm chair across from them. "Now," she said. "Tell me what this is all about. Nikki, why don't you start."

Nikki felt a flush rising up her throat. She'd never been very good at lying and tended to avoid it whenever possible. She usually found it easier to just stick to the facts, but in this case the facts were very weird. She and her mother were close, and she could usually talk with her about most things, but trying to convince her that Curio had come through a portal from another world seemed like a bad strategy. Her mother wasn't going to believe it without proof, and taking her to stare at the empty insides of an old coal boiler wasn't going to provide much evidence.

Nikki saw her mother frown and was just about to speak when a loud sniffle sounded beside her.

"It's like this, ma'am," said Curio, tears running down his cheeks. He wiped his nose with his sleeve. "My father beats me something awful. He's just a mean one, specially when he gets ale down his throat."

"Ale?" asked Mrs. Murrow in surprise.

"Beer," Nikki quickly interjected. "Curio's family is Amish, so they have weird words for things sometimes."

"Ah," said Nikki's mother, with a quick glance at Curio's woolen trousers, linen shirt, and heavy boots.

"Also, ma'am," said Curio, "he won't let me go to school, and I really wants to learn. Nikki here has taught me some things, but I really wants more book-learning. I wants to go to her place of learning."

"He means my high school," said Nikki.

"You're too young to go there," said Mrs. Murrow. "You can't be more than nine or ten."

"I'm almost eleven, ma'am, though I don't take no offence. I always been small for my age."

"Regardless," said Mrs. Murrow, "you're too young for high school and you're too young to leave your family. What about your mother? Can't she protect you from your father?"

"She's dead," said Curio ruthlessly. "And me father treats me like a servant. I won't go back there." His tear-stained face hardened into a stubbornness that Nikki was very familiar with.

"Well, what about other relatives?" asked Mrs. Murrow. "Surely you must have aunts and uncles."

"All dead," said Curio. "Terrible fever, it was. Wiped 'em all out like they was wheat at harvest time."

Mrs. Murrow shot a startled glance at Nikki, who just shrugged. Nikki knew better than to interrupt when Curio was weaving a story. He was a much better liar than she was.

"Well," said Mrs. Murrow, looking a bit shell-shocked, "why don't you stay here for tonight and we'll discuss this again tomorrow. Curio, you stay here and finish your cocoa. Nikki, come help me make up the spare bedroom."

Mrs. Murrow got sheets and blankets out of the hallway closet and led Nikki into the back bedroom. They worked in silence. When the bed was made Mrs. Murrow folded her arms and gave Nikki a stern glance. "Now, what exactly is going on?" she asked.

Nikki slapped on her best innocent expression. "What do you mean? I'm just trying to help out a friend."

Mrs. Murrow's eyebrows rose. "A friend? He's four years younger than you, and he's Amish to boot. Where did you meet him?"

"At school," said Nikki. "I noticed him hanging around in that grove of trees out behind the soccer field. I saw him there three days in a row and I started to wonder if he was homeless, so I tried to talking to him. He's quite friendly."

Mrs. Murrow laughed. "Yes, I can see that. I've never met such a smooth-talking ten-year-old."

Nikki couldn't help grinning. "Yeah, he does have a bit of the scammer in him. But he's a nice kid. He might be over-doing the 'poor me' thing, but I believe him when he says he has nowhere else to go."

"Maybe," said Mrs. Murrow. "But we can't just keep him. He has a living parent, for one thing. If I don't contact the state authorities I could possibly be charged with some kind of crime."

"Oh," said Nikki. That hadn't occurred to her. "Are you sure? I mean, we're just trying to help him."

"No, I'm not sure," said Mrs. Murrow. "Housing a homeless ten-year-old isn't something I've dealt with before. Tomorrow morning I'll go down to the Child Welfare Office, or whatever it's called. I think it's on State Street."

# Chapter Two

## Hideout

"OK, THIS WORKS," said Nikki, releasing the handle of the toilet. She and Curio were in the empty apartment below where she and her mom lived. "That's a relief. I was afraid you'd have to go back to using the bushes." She flipped the light switch in the bathroom. "The lights don't work. I guess they turned the electricity off. We haven't had any tenants in this apartment for two months. One of mom's colleagues was going to move in, but she found a cheaper place. Anyway, the lights don't matter. You can't use them anyway. My mom or old Mrs. Evanston downstairs would notice." She went into the living room and walked back and forth across the wooden floor. Loud creaking sounds echoed around the empty room.

"Maybe they won't see me," said Curio. "But ain't they gonna hear me?"

"I doubt it," said Nikki. "Old Mrs. Evanston is nearly deaf. Rocky, her malti-poo might hear you, but he's always barking about nothing. People just ignore him. And I don't think my mom will hear you. When there were people living in this apartment we couldn't hear them from upstairs." She went into the bedroom and unrolled the yoga mat and sleeping bag she'd snitched from her mom's closet. A little cloud of dust swirled up. They hadn't been used in years. "You won't exactly be living in luxury, but it'll have to do for now." She straightened up and looked Curio up and down. The T-shirt and jeans she'd bought him hung loosely on his scrawny frame and his blue eyes looked huge under the baseball cap which hid his hair. "Remember to keep that hat on. My mom gave a very accurate description of you to the social services lady. I'm not exactly sure how these things work, but social services might report you to the police as a runaway. The police might pick you up and try to return you to your parents."

"But I ain't got no parents, Miss," said Curio.

"I know," said Nikki, "but my mom thinks you do. She told social services what you said about your make-believe Dad." She looked down at Curio's feet. He was still wearing his heavy leather boots. She'd had him try on a pair of old basketball shoes in the Goodwill store, but they'd been too flimsy. His boots did a better job of supporting his fake toes and helping with his balance. "I wish we could replace those," she said, pointing at the boots. "They aren't something kids your age usually wear, and people might notice. They look like something you borrowed from your grandpa."

"Yeah," sighed Curio. "I wish I could have a pair of them fancy shoes like you're wearing, Miss." He nodded at Nikki's worn-down Nikes. "They looks real comfortable. Problem is, I don't think I could walk in them without falling over. Maybe not all the time, but enough. And people would probably notice that too."

"I have an idea about how to fix your balance problem," said Nikki. "Walking boots. They have a couple of them in the nurse's office at my high school. They're used for sprained ankles and minor breaks. They'd support your foot really well, and I think we could fit your fake toes in one. Then you could get rid of that awful leather strap that's cutting into your skin. If you leave that on much longer you're going to get an infection. I'll try to steal one of the walking boots today on my lunch break."

Curio frowned. "I don't want you stealing for me, Miss. I know I did it sometimes, back in the Realm, when I was hungry. But that was before I became a King's Emissary. Now I gots to uphold the rules."

"Fuzz is a King's Emissary and he breaks rules all the time," said Nikki.

Curio shrugged. "Yeah, Miss Athena gave me a very long talking-to about that. She said Mr. Fuzz is not a person I should be modeling myself after and I needs to hold myself to a higher standard."

"Well, in this case we'll just have to lower our standards," said Nikki. "Your foot is bleeding from that leather strap and I know it's hurting you. I'm not a big fan of stealing either, but in this case I think we have a good reason."

She went over to the bedroom window and opened it. "I don't think you'll have any trouble getting in and out of here. You can't use the front door, obviously, but these ivy vines are really old and thick. Let's try it." She sat on the windowsill and swung her legs out, grasping the ivy vines with both hands. The shiny green leaves were slippery, and some of the vines were too weak and broke off under her hands, but she managed to find the weight-bearing vines and scrambled down to wait on the damp grass for Curio. His usual monkey-like agility was hampered by his foot injury, but he climbed down the vines without too much trouble.

"I don't think anyone will see you in here," said Nikki, glancing around the small side-yard of the building, which was surrounded by a ten-foot yew hedge. "You won't be able to use the gate, but there's a gap under the hedge, right over here. I think someone's dog dug it." She lay down on the grass on her stomach and pulled herself under the hedge using her elbows. "Come on," she said as Curio joined her on the sidewalk. "We can't hang around here. Someone might see you." She led the way quickly down a side street toward Lake Monona.

"I'm sorry about all this, Miss," said Curio. "I hope I ain't gonna get you in no trouble."

"Don't worry about it," said Nikki. "I don't think my mom's mad. She was just startled when she found out you were gone this morning. I hated to upset her, but I had to get you out of there. She was dead set on taking you to the social services office."

"Yeah," said Curio. "I can't be bothering with Serving Offices right now. I needs to be hunting down Rufius so I can report back to Mr. Fuzz and Miss Athena soon as the portal opens again."

"Over here," said Nikki when they reached the lakeshore. She sat down on a picnic table. Cooing pigeons immediately swarmed in, hoping for a handout. Out on the choppy water a fleet of one-person sailboats was tacking between bright red buoys. Across the lake the white dome of the Wisconsin State Capital building shone in the morning sun.

"So," said Nikki, "as far as the search goes, I think we should start at my high school and work outwards from there. That's how the police here do it. They're kind of like the Rounders back in the Realm of Reason. They set up a perimeter, like a five-mile radius from a center point. My guess is that our perimeter will be a lot smaller than that. Rufius is a complete stranger to this world, just like you. He's going to have a hard time adjusting to a lot of things. I'm guessing he'll stay close to the portal."

Curio nodded. "And he'll probably change clothes," he said, picking at a hole in his jeans. "He'll get rid of that silly black tunic he always wears and get himself some of these strange pants." He lifted his T-shirt and fiddled with the zipper of his jeans. "Miss, what is this thing, and how does it hold up me pants? I never seen anything like it before."

"Stop doing that," said Nikki. "It isn't polite behavior in public."

"Sorry, Miss," said Curio, a red flush rising up his pale neck. He quickly pulled his T-shirt back down.

They sat silently watching the sailboats for a few minutes, each lost in their own thoughts. Curio finally broke the silence.

"Miss, why don't you just leave the Rufius-finding to me? He's our problem, after all. Not yours. He's the Realm's responsibility. Miss Athena and Mr. Fuzz would agree with me. They'd be mortified if you had to fix our mistake. Rufius shoulda been grabbed and thrown in the Castle Cogent dungeon before Mr. Bertie's coronation, but the problem was nobody could find him. He's a slippery devil. All the numbskulls working with him to overthrow the Realm, all them Knights of the Iron Fist, they been rounded up and either dumped in dungeons or kicked out of the Realm. The Prince of Physics himself saw to that. And he also tried to track Rufius down, but no luck. Problem was we didn't know that he'd slipped through the portal until quite a while afterward."

"I wonder why he did," said Nikki. "Go through the portal, I mean. I get that he wanted to avoid capture, but coming to another world was a huge risk. I know I did it a year ago, but I think that's because I'd been sitting in that janitor's closet too long and I was off my head from breathing all those cleaning fluids."

Curio shrugged. "I dunno. I might have done the same thing as Rufius. You gotta understand, Miss. There were a lot of people in the Realm who wanted to hang him. Hanging's not a common thing in the Realm, but it does happen sometimes. For really serious crimes. And it's hard to imagine a crime more serious than trying to overthrow the entire Realm. And he knew that Mr. Fuzz and Miss Athena were sending you through the portal back to your own land. They wouldn't have done that if it wasn't pretty safe."

"Yeah," said Nikki. "But it's not entirely reliable. I remember Fuzz mentioned once that he'd gone through the portal and ended up in a completely unfamiliar world."

Curio nodded. "The one with that sheep that followed him through. He had to chase it down and wrestle it back through the portal cause it didn't want to go back to the Realm."

"Right," said Nikki. "Anyway, Rufius took a big chance coming here. There's a lot here he's going to be completely unfamiliar with. So I think our best chance of getting him back to the Realm is to find him really fast, before he learns how to get along in this world."

Curio hopped off the picnic table. "Then let's get started, Miss. Back to your place of learning."

Nikki pulled her phone out of her pocket to check the time. "It's too early. My school won't be open until nine. My mom dragged me out of bed and down to the Social Services office at 7 am this morning when she found out you were gone. The office wasn't even open, but she banged on the door until someone came."

"Well, if we can't get into your place of learning yet then let's just walk around that perimeter thing you mentioned," said Curio. "Maybe we'll spot Rufius."

"All right," said Nikki. "But no confronting him if we spot him. Promise me."

Curio's thin face tightened into stubbornness under his baseball cap. "But Miss, I really needs to kick him, and kick him hard. The whole Realm wants to kick him."

"I know," said Nikki. "But he's twice your size. If you kick him he might kill you."

Curio muttered something that didn't sound much like a no-kicking promise, but Nikki let it go. She left the lakeside and led Curio quickly along the crowded sidewalks in downtown Madison where people were rushing to work or to the University of Wisconsin nearby. They arrived at her high school just as a guard was unlocking the front doors.

"Let's start over there," said Nikki, pointing to a grove of trees behind the soccer field. "It's close to the school but kind of hidden. Rufius might have camped out among the trees."

"Rufius is more of a feather-bed kind of person," said Curio. "I can't see him sleeping on the ground."

"He might not have a choice right now," said Nikki. "He's in a strange world without any money. Not any of our money, at least. Gold coins from the Realm won't do him much good . . ." She stopped, lost in thought.

"What is it, Miss?" asked Curio.

"Gold coins," said Nikki. "The official coins, the ones from the Castle Cogent treasury, they're almost pure gold. There are places here where you can trade gold for the type of money we use in this world. They're called pawnshops. If Rufius finds one and figures out how to trade gold for cash that could be really bad. He'd have a much easier time here in this world. Money makes everything easier." She abruptly turned on her heel and headed back toward downtown. "There's a pawnshop not far from here. On State Street, near the capital building."

The rush hour traffic and sidewalk crowds increased as they walked, but it didn't take long to locate the pawnshop. It was a tiny ground-floor shop in a crumbling ten-story building that had been built nearly a century ago and badly needed a facelift. The shop's front window hadn't been washed in years and the jumbled contents were barely visible. Nikki spotted a few cheap glass vases, a fake Tiffany lamp, and a pile of dusty old pennies. A bell jangled as she opened the door.

"Out!" a voice yelled. "We don't serve kids here. You try to shoplift and I'll call the police.

Nikki smiled at the man behind the counter. He looked eighty and could barely see over the cash register. "We're just looking for our father," she said. "He might have been in here trying to trade some gold coins. He said he could get good money for them, but he hasn't been back home in days and we're out of food. My little brother's hungry." She nudged Curio, who sniffed a pitiful-orphan sniff and stared down at the floor.

The man eyed them up and down, but finally nodded. "Yeah, there was a man in here yesterday who had some gold coins. Real strange ones. I still haven't figured out what country they're from. What'd he look like, your father?"

"He's pretty tall," said Nikki, stretching her hand above her head. "With black hair and real pale skin. He looks real young for his age. Everyone comments on it."

"Yeah," said the old man. "I was just thinking the customer with the coins is too young to be your father. How old are you?"

"I'm fourteen," said Nikki. "My father had me when he was only fifteen. He's twenty-nine now but looks a lot younger."

"Hmm," said the old man, scrabbling in a drawer under the counter. He held out a coin for Nikki to see. "This look familiar?"

Nikki nodded. "I think so. Dad didn't let us touch the coins, so it's hard to say for sure. He used to keep them in a shoebox in his closet. He said his grandpa left them to him."

"So you don't know what kind they are?" asked the old man, sounding disappointed. "I tried looking them up in The Numismatist and Coin World, but I couldn't find anything even close."

"Sorry," said Nikki. "We don't know what they are, just that they're gold."

"Yeah, they're gold all right," said the old man, turning the coin over in his palm. "I gave your dad a fair price for the gold content. Nothing more. He might have got a better deal at a coin shop. There's Dawson's shop, two blocks over. They specialize in old coins. You tell him that, next time you see him." He paused, staring at Curio, who was still looking at the floor and sniffling. The old man sighed. He opened the cash register and pulled out a twenty-dollar bill, handing it to Nikki. "Go buy some groceries. And get that kid some Kleenex."

Nikki thanked him and hustled Curio out of the shop. "Well, Rufius now has money," she said. "I wanted to ask the pawnbroker how much money he gave him, but I was afraid that would make him suspicious."

"That's money, Miss?" asked Curio, looking dubiously at the twenty-dollar bill. "It's just a piece of green paper. Money is made out of metal."

Nikki pulled a quarter out of the pocket of her jeans. "We have metal coins here, just like you do in the Realm, but they're not very valuable. For larger amounts we use these pieces of paper. They're easier to carry around."

"If you say so, Miss," said Curio, still looking unconvinced. "So, now what? Back to your place of learning?"

"I'm not sure," said Nikki, thoughtfully turning the twenty-dollar bill over in her hand. "Where Rufius is depends on how much money he got from the pawnbroker. If he got hundreds of dollars then he can afford to sleep indoors in a cheap hotel. Or at the YMCA. At least for a week or so. But just locking himself in a room for a week doesn't seem like something he'd do. Even in a strange and unfamiliar world I think his instinct for scheming would get the better of him."

She headed back down State Street towards her high school. "Come on. I'll buy you breakfast and then I've got to get to class. I'm late already. If I don't show up my home-room teacher will call my mother. You can go back to the empty apartment and take a nap. Just be careful not to let anyone see you. I get out of school around three in the afternoon. Keep the bedroom window unlocked so I can get in. And keep the chain on the front door. That way you'll have time to climb out the window if anyone comes by. I don't think anyone will, but it's possible the landlord might try to show the apartment to a new tenant."

# Chapter Three

## Sighting

IT WAS HIS posture which attracted her attention. Nikki slowed down, ignoring the students rushing down the hall all around her. She peered around a tall boy walking in front of her. The hair was the right color, a very dark black. And the neck poking out from a grubby janitor's jumpsuit was extremely pale. But it was the posture which stood out. Rigidly straight shoulders, a ramrod back. The head tilted up, not bent in the tired, overworked way of a blue-collar worker in a tough job. But she couldn't be sure. Not until she saw his face, and she didn't know how to do that without him spotting her. A sudden shove from behind startled her.

"Come on Nikki," said Tina, the captain of the school's debate team. She gave Nikki another push with one hand while running a brush through her red hair with the other. "Get a move on or we'll be late for class. Lateness makes the whole team look bad."

"Stop pushing, Tina," Nikki snapped. Up ahead the figure in the janitor's uniform had disappeared. She tried to ignore her uneasiness and followed Tina into their debate class.

"Nikki, Tina, you're late. Take a seat," barked Mr. Tomlinson from behind his desk. "Debate Team members are supposed to set a good example for the rest of the class. You're not starting off the semester in a stellar manner."

Most of the students snickered. Debate was a required class for all seniors at Westlake High, so most of the large class didn't want to be there. And Mr. Tomlinson both favored and relentlessly criticized the students who were on the debate team. This made the team members extremely unpopular. Nikki had learned to shrug off the catcalls and the occasional pencil thrown at her head, but it did make the class less than pleasant. It didn't help that Tina constantly bullied the other team members into wearing their Westlake Debate Team t-shirts in class. Nikki didn't usually comply, but she was wearing hers today because she hadn't really been paying attention when she'd gotten dressed that morning, what with her worries about Curio.

Mr. Tomlinson shoved his chair back and stood up. He smoothed a thin patch of grey hair over his bald spot and pointed at the chalkboard. "Today we'll be discussing the Appeal to Nature fallacy. Now, who knows what it is?"

Everyone in the class immediately looked at Tina, and sure enough, her hand shot up.

"The Appeal to Nature fallacy is the idea that everything in nature is good," said Tina.

"Close enough," said Mr. Tomlinson. "Nikki," he barked, "why is this a fallacy? After all, nature is fluffy kittens, daisies, and meadows in spring. Every laundry commercial on television says so."

"Well," said Nikki. "Nature does have lots of good things, but it also has lots of bad ones. Bad for humans, I mean. There are lots of natural things which are harmful to us, like bacteria, viruses, poisonous snakes, scorpions, flash floods, hurricanes, wildfires, tornados. It's a long list. The Appeal to Nature fallacy ignores all this bad stuff. The fallacy is really common among people in the dietary supplement industry. Both the people who sell supplements and the people who buy them. They think that things like plant extracts and essential oils and all that stuff are better for them than something made in a laboratory. But lots of plants are dangerous. Comfrey extract can damage your liver, for instance. And eating foxglove can cause heart attacks. Even a really common plant like oleander is poisonous to humans. There's a bit of wishful thinking involved and more than a little ego. People who commit this fallacy say that nature is good and beautiful and provides for all our needs and is never capable of hurting us. But nature, the earth, and the universe all existed long before our humanoid ancestors arrived on the scene. It's ridiculously egotistical to think that nature exists only to serve human needs."

"Murrow, you talk too much," someone shouted from the back of the class.

"You forgot ought-is," said Tina, throwing a smug glance at Nikki.

"Elaborate," barked Mr. Tomlinson.

Tina cleared her throat. "The ought-is problem was first introduced by the Scottish philosopher David Hume in his book *The Treatise of Human Nature*, first published in 1739 . . ."

"We don't need a history lesson," snapped Mr. Tomlinson. "Kindly relate ought-is to the Appeal to Nature fallacy or let someone else take the floor."

"The Appeal to Nature fallacy has a strong current of "ought" underlying it," said Tina. "As in, we "ought" to eat only so-called natural foods. The idea being that natural foods are not only healthier for us, but that people who eat natural foods are physically and even morally superior to people who eat processed foods. So, the Appeal to Nature fallacy generates prescriptive statements about what ought to be."

"Hmm," said Mr. Tomlinson. "Not bad. Rebuttals?"

"I think Tina's confusing the Appeal to Nature fallacy with the Naturalistic Fallacy," said Nikki.

"I am not," hissed Tina, throwing Nikki a death stare. "And you still haven't paid me for the silk shirt you ruined when you spilled Coke on it."

"I'm saving my allowance for it," said Nikki. "I don't have enough money yet. Anyway, the main point of the Naturalistic Fallacy, also called the ought-is problem, is that you can't come to a moral conclusion from non-moral premises. Ought refers to morality, while Is refers to observable facts about the world. The Naturalistic Fallacy is sometimes called NOFI. No Ought from Is. It's similar to an algebraic equation." A loud groan erupted from the back of the class but Nikki ignored it. "If you multiply one side of an algebraic equation by the number ten, then you have to multiply the other side by ten. It's a mathematical axiom that equations have to be balanced. Anything you do to one side you have to do to the other. If you don't then the equation is unbalanced. With NOFI, by introducing morality into only one side you're making the philosophical equation unbalanced."

"Hmm," said Mr. Tomlinson. "I'm not generally a fan of introducing mathematics into a philosophical argument. You risk losing people who don't have a mathematical background, and you also run the risk of moving into formal logic territory. This class focuses on informal logic. If you want to impress people with modus ponens or propositional calculus then I suggest you do so on your own time, Murrow. Now, homework. Everyone write a one-page essay on the Appeal to Nature fallacy. Use the rest of the class time to get started on it. Three-hundred words, minimum."

Nikki settled down to work. She was halfway through her essay when there was a knock on the classroom door. She looked up to see Rufius standing in the doorway. He nodded to Mr. Tomlinson and picked up the wastebasket next to the chalkboard. When he returned with the empty wastebasket he gave Nikki a barely noticeable wink before sauntering out.

The girl sitting behind her let out a long sigh. "Oh my gosh. I've never seen a janitor looking as good as that. I don't even care that he probably makes minimum wage."

"Back to work!" snapped Mr. Tomlinson. "No talking."

When the bell rang to signal the end of class Nikki jumped up immediately. She wanted to leave in the middle of a crush of students, just in case Rufius was hanging around outside the classroom. Unfortunately Mr. Tomlinson had other ideas.

"Nikki, Tina," he barked. "Hang back. I want to discuss our upcoming debate with Southside High. We need to finalize the speaker lineup."

Tina and Mr. Tomlinson immediately launched into a heated discussion about who would be the first affirmative speaker on their team and who would be the second. Nikki stayed quiet in the hope that they'd finish sooner, but by the time they resolved things to Tina's satisfaction the bell for the start of the next class had rung and the hallways were completely empty.

"Tina, walk with me to my chemistry class," said Nikki. "We can talk about the debate on the way."

"Don't be ridiculous," snapped Tina. "I'm already late for Spanish and it's in the opposite direction." She rushed away down the hall, checking her eyeshadow in a compact mirror as she walked.

Nikki looked right and left. No sign of Rufius. She headed for her chemistry class at a jog. She didn't really think she was in any danger during the middle of the school day, but she still didn't want an encounter with Rufius on her own. As she ran past the janitor's closet which held the portal to the Realm of Reason she came to a sudden halt. An extremely odd noise was coming out of the closet. Nikki couldn't make out what it was, but it didn't sound human. A bead of sweat dripped down her back as she grasped the door handle and slowly turned it. Furious banging came from the other side of the door and it swung open with a crash.

A fluffy white sheep charged out of the closet and skidded on the linoleum floor. It slid head-first into a bank of lockers with a metallic clatter. Its short, curved horns got stuck in the door of a locker and its back hooves flailed like a pickup-truck stuck in heavy snow as it tried to pull its head free. The sheep let out a loud bleat of panic and twisted back and forth.

Nikki grabbed its hind quarters and pulled. A painful kick in the shin from a hoof convinced her that this wasn't a great idea. Still, she couldn't leave a Realm of Reason sheep wandering around her high school. She had no idea what the consequences might be, but she remembered Fuzz's wrestling match with another sheep which had wandered through the portal. He'd seemed pretty certain that leaving Realm sheep to wander around other worlds was not the thing to do. Assuming this *was* a Realm sheep and not just another prank by the varsity football team. Last week they'd dumped a bucket full of live trout into the school's swimming pool.

Nikki gave up on pulling the sheep loose and darted to the closet door, taking a quick look inside. No Rufius. No other janitors. She spotted the battered toolbox she'd seen on her last visit to the closet. Throwing open its lid she grabbed a hammer and ran back to the sheep. The claw end of the hammer bent the thin metal of the locker as if it was tinfoil. The sheep pulled its horns free and made a dash for freedom. Nikki dropped the hammer and threw herself across its back, but was shocked to find that this had no effect whatsoever on the sheep. Instead she found herself carried down the hallway like a kid on a pony ride. The sheep charged like a linebacker straight through a partially open door and burst out onto the soccer field at the back of the school.

"Ride that thing, Murrow," shouted one of the boys on the varsity soccer team as the sheep ran full tilt through their scrimmage, head-butting the players not quick enough to dodge out of its way.

Nikki felt a soccer ball bounce off her head as the sheep crossed the field and ran into a small grove of oak trees behind the school. The loud hoots of laughter gradually faded as the trees crowded in and years of fallen leaves slowed the sheep's progress. It finally came to a wheezing halt and Nikki slid off, clutching her aching ribs. She kept one hand on the sheep, her fingers tightly gripping its thick wool.

"Now what?" she said to the sheep, which was rooting among the fallen oak leaves for anything edible.

"You should really return that sheep to Lansdale farm," said a creaky voice.

Nikki gasped and spun around.

A shadowy form that looked like a pile of old rags emerged from behind an oak tree.

"Fortuna?" Nikki whispered.

"One and the same, dearie," croaked Fortuna the Fortunate. She grinned, showing off her missing teeth to grotesque effect.

"What . . . how . . .how did you get here?" Nikki stammered.

"Same way that sheep did," said Fortuna, shrugging. "I just followed it through the wall. Heard a rumor about that wall. People all over Cogent Town were talking about it. So I just waited in that alley until something happened. And sure enough, something did. That sheep wandered in, bumped up against the wall, and just sorta melted through. I put my hand through the same spot on the wall, and before I knew it the rest of me followed." She pointed at a patch of smooth skin on the sheep's back where the wool had been sheared. A blue 'L' was painted there. "That's the Lansdale mark. Their sheep are always running around loose in Cogent Town cause they don't keep their fences in good order."

Nikki just stared at the old woman, a dozen things running through her mind. First Rufius, then the sheep, now Fortuna. Was the entire population of the Realm of Reason, both human and animal, going to come through the portal? She wondered if she should try to block up the portal somehow. Maybe put a lock on the door of the old boiler in the janitor's closet. But that might prevent Fuzz and Athena from getting through, and she desperately wanted them to come and help her with the Rufius problem. And now she had a Fortuna problem as well. Fortuna wasn't as dangerous as Rufius, at least not physically, but she had the same scammy lack of ethics and plenty of potential to cause problems all on her own.

"So, where am I?" asked Fortuna. "Is this your world, or a different one entirely? Not that I really care. Any place is better for me than the Realm right now. It's a little too hot for me there, if you know what I mean. Lots of people in Cogent Town are clamoring for my head, just because I lifted a bit of gold here and there. Just a few coins, not enough for anyone to miss. I mean, a poor old woman's got to eat. But they're saying I was in on the plans Rufius made to take over the Realm. Nothing doing. I knows not to get involved with such nonsense. Yeah, maybe I did a bit of business with him in D-ville. Bit of potion-selling. We both made a nice fat profit outta that. But selling a few harmless potions to the nobles is a long way from trying to take down the King. Anyway, fair or not, I had to get outta town before they threw me in the Castle Cogent dungeons, and I didn't have the money for the long trip back to D-ville. This sheep was me savior." She slapped the sheep on its woolly rump and the sheep let out a loud, irritated bleat.

"So, dearie," said Fortuna, "got any coin on ya? Just a bit of gold to tide me over while I gets me bearings in this here world. You owe me, you know. That little stunt you pulled on the Isle of Ignorance cost me dearly. Ruined my Fish Fortunes business. The locals never trusted my predictions after that. I had to start all over again in D-ville. It ain't easy starting over again at my age." Her sagging face hardened and she stuck out a withered hand.

Nikki shook her head. "Nope. I owe you nothing. You were cheating those people with your silly Fish Fortunes and I'm glad I ruined your so-called business. Now, you need to go back to the Realm immediately. Come on."

Fortuna just laughed and spat on the ground. "You ain't got no right to order me around, little girl. I'll go where I like." She spun on her heel and tottered off, deeper into the oak grove.

Nikki watched her go. There was nothing she could do. And Rufius was the bigger problem. She couldn't waste time following Fortuna around. She sighed and looked down at the sheep, wondering how on earth Fuzz had managed to wrestle one all on his own. The sheep looked up at her, its mouth full of muddy oak leaves. It seemed to give her a saucy wink, as if it knew very well that in this battle between human and sheep, the sheep had emerged victorious. It waddled slowly off into the shadows of the oak grove in the same direction as Fortuna, leaving Nikki to throw her hands up in defeat.

# Chapter Four

## Burrowing In

MRS. MURROW OPENED the Wisconsin State Journal to the local news page and shoved it across the dinner table to Nikki. "Your school nearly had to hire a new principal," she said, tapping the newspaper with her fork.

Nikki glanced down at the paper. 'School janitor saves life of principal' read the headline. She quickly skimmed the article. Mr. Randall, the principal of her high school, had been kayaking on Lake Mendota near the campus of the University of Wisconsin when he'd capsized. A man referred to only as 'Bill' had pulled the unconscious principal out of the water. An emergency medic on the scene had speculated that the principal may have had a stroke, which caused him to blackout and fall into the water.

"Hmm," murmured Nikki, reading through the short article again. There was nothing in the article which was out of the ordinary, but the butterflies which had flitted around in her stomach ever since Rufius had come through the portal were swarming madly again. Mr. Randall was sixty-seven. She knew his age because they'd announced his birthday over the school intercom a few weeks ago. A stroke at his age was not unusual, so that checked out. But it was the words 'school janitor' in the headline which set her nerves on edge. The article didn't specify that the janitor worked at Westlake High, but still . . .

"Don't look so worried," said her mother. "I'm sure your principal will be fine."

"Yeah, of course," said Nikki. "I'm sure he'll be okay." She pushed the paper away and jumped up to clear the table. She carried her soup bowl into the kitchen and loaded it into the dishwasher. Then she snagged a packet of sliced turkey from the fridge. She shoved it down her jeans and covered it with her t-shirt. She grabbed a handful of chocolate-covered almonds from a ceramic bowl on the counter and stuffed them into her pocket. "I'm just going to run downstairs," she called from the kitchen. "Mrs. Evanston wants my help moving a bookcase. I won't be long." She grabbed the paper grocery bag she'd stashed in the front closet and rushed out before her mother had a chance to reply.

She ran down the stairs and knocked softly on the door of the second-floor apartment. "Curio, it's me," she whispered. "Open up."

The door-chain rattled and Curio poked his head out. "Hello, Miss. I didn't expect you until morning."

"I know," said Nikki, slipping inside and shutting the door. "But I managed to grab some food for you from our kitchen." She put the packet of turkey on the dusty kitchen counter and looked around for something to put the almonds in. The landlord had done a thorough job of clearing out the cupboards so she pulled a piece of toilet paper off the roll in the bathroom and put the partly melted almonds on that. "Sorry," she said. "I know it's not the most exciting dinner, but it was the best I could do."

"It's wonderful, Miss," said Curio, stuffing his face with almonds.

While he ate Nikki went over to the radiator and turned it on. She was relieved to hear a quiet rattle and the hiss of steam. It was late September and Madison's famously cold weather always got an early start. The city sometimes got snow as early as October.

"We're going to have to go to Goodwill again," she said. "If you're determined to stay here you'll need a winter coat soon. If you pull out all the stops on your pathetic-orphan routine they might give you a coat for free."

Curio wiped his chocolate-covered mouth on the sleeve of his t-shirt and ripped open the packet of turkey. "Sure, Miss," he said with his mouth full. "Whatever you say."

"I saw Rufius," said Nikki.

Curio choked on a piece of turkey. He ran to the bathroom and spit into the toilet. When he came out he gave Nikki an irritated look. "Give me a warning next time you has news like that, Miss. I nearly swallowed me tongue."

"Sorry," said Nikki. "Anyway, he somehow got a job as a janitor at my school. He came into one of my classes to empty the trash can and looked right at me. And to make matters worse, Fortuna the Fortunate is here too."

"Oh," said Curio, stuffing another piece of turkey in his mouth. "That's not good, but it's not the end of the world, Miss. Old Fortuna's more a nuisance than a threat, I'd say."

"Maybe," said Nikki, "but she can cause a lot of trouble when she wants to. We should keep an eye on her. I was thinking you could help with that. She wandered off into the woods behind my school. Tomorrow you could try to find out where she's gone. I think she'll have a harder time surviving in this world than Rufius will. Rufius has some big advantages, like youth, looks, and charisma. Those were all it took for him to gather hundreds of followers in the Realm. Fortuna has none of those qualities. If things get too hard for her here we might be able to convince her to go back through the portal."

Curio shrugged. "Okay, Miss. But I still thinks Rufius is the one we should focus on. The quicker we can get him back to the Realm the less damage he can do here in your world."

"I agree," said Nikki. "But since we can't open the portal on command we have no way to get him back through it. Until it opens we'll just have to keep an eye on him. And since you don't go to my school you can't just wander around it. So I'll have to take Rufius and you take Fortuna."

She retrieved the paper grocery bag from where she'd left it by the front door. "This is the walking boot I told you about. I snitched it from the nurse's station at school. They had a couple of sizes and I got the smallest. Let's try it on."

Curio pulled off his heavy leather boot and stuck his injured foot into the plastic walking boot. Nikki helped him tighten the Velcro straps.

"It's not too bad, Miss," said Curio, clumping around the living room. It's better than me old boot, but I still lists to one side, so to speak."

"Yeah, I can see that," said Nikki. She pulled a pair of scissors out of the grocery bag. "Let's try it with the leg of your jeans outside the boot." She unstrapped the boot and cut the leg of Curio's jeans up to the knee. This time she pulled the Velcro straps much tighter.

"Oh, that's very good, Miss," said Curio. "I can walk almost normal again. What's all this squishy stuff inside? It's very comfy."

"That called foam," said Nikki. "It's molding itself to your foot and holding it in place. You should be all set. Just remember to take the boot off every night to prevent circulation problems."

Nikki collected the grocery bag and the empty turkey packet. "I have to get back before my mom wonders where I am. Let's meet up in the woods behind my school tomorrow, late in the afternoon. My classes will be over by then. We can compare notes."

NIKKI STARED OPEN-MOUTHED at the notice on the school bulletin board. The picture was fuzzy, but it was definitely Rufius. The caption under the picture read 'Please welcome Westlake High's newest guidance counselor, Bill Radnor'.

She briefly wondered where he'd come up with the name Radnor, but more importantly, how the heck had he gone from being a janitor for only one day to suddenly becoming a high school guidance counselor? Whoever had hired him must not care at all about qualifications. She had a strong suspicion that it had something to do with the school's principal almost drowning in Lake Mendota. 'Bill' had obviously been on the spot, but had 'Bill' just done the saving, or had he also caused the drowning? The Rufius she'd known in the Realm of Reason had usually gotten other people to do any actual violence, but he was definitely capable of it. It wouldn't have taken much effort for him to tip over the kayak of an elderly man and then hold him underwater.

Nikki pulled the picture off the bulletin board and tucked it in her backpack. Having a picture of Rufius might come in handy. She wondered what he'd thought about his first experience with a camera and the sight of his own photograph. It had to have been a bit of a shock, but he had the same kind of intense adaptability that Curio had. His lack of experience in this world wasn't going to be as much of a hindrance to him as she'd hoped.

The bell rang, reminding her that she was about to be late for her chemistry class. She darted through the stragglers in the hall and slipped through the classroom door just as Mrs. Halford was closing it. The classroom was set up with rows of lab stations instead of desks. Nikki hopped onto her usual stool and plopped her backpack between her assigned microscope and a small sink which she shared with her lab partner. Who, unfortunately, was Tina. Tina was taking all the same AP classes, and her last name was Moore, which always put her right next to Nikki in the classroom roll-call lists and seating assignments.

"Nikki," whispered Tina, poking Nikki in the arm with a pencil. "Is this Lewis structure of NaCl right?"

Nikki glanced at Tina's paper. "The octet's right, but you forgot the charges."

"Blast it," whispered Tina, quickly adding a plus sign above the Na symbol for sodium and a negative sign above the Cl symbol for chlorine.

"All right class," said Mrs. Halford, "pass your homework forward."

Nikki swiveled on her stool to collect the paper from the student behind her, and that was when she spotted him. Rufius was huddled with two boys sitting in the back row.

Mrs. Halford spotted him at the same time. "Mr. Radnor, is it? I realize you're new here, but as a rule our guidance counselors do not conduct their business in the classroom. It is highly disruptive. Please leave at once." She brushed a speck of dust off the sleeve of her severely tailored gray suit and aimed a cold stare at Rufius over the top of her bifocals.

"Of course, ma'am," said Rufius, flashing his most charming smile. "My apologies. I'm afraid I just got caught up in my new duties. I feel an obligation to get to know each and every student in the school."

"Well, get to know them somewhere other than my chemistry class," snapped Mrs. Halford, looking not the least bit charmed.

Nikki stifled a laugh. Sometimes Mrs. Halford reminded her strongly of Athena, that imp of spotless gray dresses and steel-plated backbone.

Rufius strolled down the rows, smiling at the students and shaking hands like a politician stumping for votes. Nikki thought he was overdoing it, but she noticed that some of the girls were clinging to his hand a bit too long. His striking looks, with his very pale skin and black hair were definitely a weapon he could wield when he chose to. He was wearing a tight-fitting purple suit which looked like it had last been fashionable back in the sixties, yet it looked custom-made for him, with just a hint of rock star.

"What a poser," whispered Tina.

Nikki snorted with laughter. Good old Tina. She was a perpetual pain in the ass, but she wasn't a fool.

"Now class," said Mrs. Halford once the door had closed on Rufius, "We will be doing separation of a dye mixture using chromatography. There are chromatography strips in the drawers under your lab stations. Please bring a small beaker up to my desk to receive the dye mixture. You will also need a 250 milliliter Erlenmeyer flask and a watch glass. This experiment uses capillary action to separate and identify the substances in a mixture."

Nikki tried to put Rufius out of her mind and concentrate on the experiment. But at the end of the class, after she'd turned in her results, she headed for the back of the room.

"Hey Tom," she said, climbing onto an empty stool next to a scrawny, sandy-haired boy who was working the chromatography experiment on his own. "Where's your lab partner?"

Tom shrugged. "Don't know. Sick probably."

Nikki casually looked over her shoulder at the two boys in the back row. They were having an intense, whispered argument about something and didn't even glance in her direction. "So, Tom, did you happen to hear what the new guidance counselor was saying to those idiots behind you?"

Tom's shoulders immediately rose up to his ears.

"So you *did* hear," said Nikki. "What was it?"

Tom stood rigid and still, one hand clutching an Erlenmeyer flask.

Nikki waited.

Finally Tom whispered something. It was so faint that Nikki couldn't catch it.

"What?" she said.

"Phenylacetone," whispered Tom. "The guidance counselor wanted to know if they could get some."

Nikki gasped. Phenylacetone was a starting ingredient for meth. "Are you sure that's what he said?" she asked.

"Yep," said Tom. "Now go away. I ain't saying no more about it. I've got nothing to do with those jerks and I want to keep it that way."

Nikki slid off the stool and returned to her lab station. She absentmindedly washed her beakers and flasks, then collected her things and followed the rest of the class out when the bell rang for lunch. She headed out to her usual bench on the edge of the soccer field and pulled a sack lunch out of her backpack. She ate the chicken salad sandwich her mom had made and turned the startling events of the chemistry class over in her mind.

It had to be TV. Rufius must have seen a news report about meth on TV, maybe in a bar, or maybe he was staying at the YMCA and they had a TV in the lobby. He wouldn't have known what a TV was, but he would have understood the words and the pictures well enough. His world and the modern world of Madison, Wisconsin shared a common language. English. It was a bizarre common denominator which Nikki had never understood. She'd mulled it over many times in the weeks since returning from the Realm, but had never come to any conclusion. She shoved the mystery back into its place in her subconscious and returned to more pressing problems. Like how she was going to stop Rufius from using a couple of nitwits in her chemistry class to start a meth lab. If they succeeded in creating the drug they'd probably try to sell it to the students at Westlake High. She couldn't let that happen. Meth was a horrific drug. It could ruin people's lives very quickly.

"Hi, Miss," said Curio, plopping down on the bench beside her.

"Oh, hi," said Nikki. "You startled me. I wasn't expecting you until later."

"I remembered you said you took your midday meal out here," said Curio. "So I thought I'd try to catch you, cause I has some news."

Nikki dug into her sack lunch and pulled out another sandwich. "Here. I told my mom I was really hungry today and she made me two."

"Thanks, Miss," said Curio through a mouthful of chicken salad. "Me news is about Fortuna. I tried looking for her in the woods where you spotted her, but couldn't find no trace of her. So I just wandered about for a bit. I didn't really have a plan, so I just walked along that big street with all the iron monsters going up and down it. Where we was yesterday."

"Iron monsters?" said Nikki.

"Yeah," said Curio. "Them things that go faster than any horse and look like they want to flatten you into a pancake."

"Oh," said Nikki. "Cars."

"Yeah. Them. Anyway, I was walking near that place where you asked that man about gold coins. And who should I spot, but old Fortuna herself. She was coming out the door of a little shop with red velvet curtains in the windows. It had the word 'Psychic' in big gold letters on the door. What does that mean, anyway? I ain't never come across the word before."

"It's kind of like a fortune teller," said Nikki. "Which makes sense. When Fuzz, Athena and I were on the Isle of Ignorance Fortuna was running a scam called Fish Fortunes. She was using this big tank full of tropical fish to tell people's fortunes. Total nonsense of course, but you gotta give her points for originality."

"I didn't see no fish in this shop," said Curio. "There was just a woman sitting at a table. Kind of ordinary looking, except she had these really long fingernails with little green stars painted on them. She had a bunch of cards laid out in front of her with funny pictures on them. She said they was Staro cards or something."

"Tarot cards," said Nikki.

"Right. Anyways, I asked her if she knew the old woman who'd just left and she said sure. Turns out she'd hired old Fortuna as a fortune teller. She even gave her a cot at the back of the shop to sleep on."

"Huh," said Nikki. "Well, I don't see how Fortuna can cause much trouble just telling fortunes. Downtown Madison isn't the Isle of Ignorance. On the Isle people were really, desperately poor. They couldn't afford to lose the money Fortuna was scamming them out of. But Madison isn't a poor city. Most people here can afford to lose a few dollars to a psychic if they're dumb enough to go to one. I guess we can just let Fortuna be for now. If Fuzz, Athena, or any castle guards come through the portal we can tell them where she is so they can take her back to the Realm. If she starts trying to sell dangerous potions or something like that we might have to interfere, but for now we need to concentrate on Rufius. He's gotten involved in some very dangerous stuff, and he's settling into this world a lot faster than I'd hoped. The worst of it is he's gotten students involved in his plans. That's probably why he wrangled that job as a guidance counselor. It gives him more access to students than a janitor would have. Not every student in this school is an idiot, of course. Tina saw right through him. But he does have that John Travolta in Grease sort of charisma. Some of the more gullible kids are gonna follow him around like puppies."

"Who's John Travolta?" asked Curio.

"An actor," said Nikki. "He plays a part, to entertain people."

"Oh," said Curio. "Yeah, we have those too. We call them players. They can collect a lot of followers, but I don't recall any of them getting involved in Rufius's revolt against the King. Players mostly spend all their time drinking ale and buying fancy clothes." He shot a quick glance at Nikki, who was staring intently down at the grass of the soccer field. "Is something wrong, Miss?" Curio asked.

Nikki shook her head. "No. I was just trying to figure out our next move. I was wondering if we could get Rufius fired from his new job. That might not stop him from hatching dangerous plans, but at least it might get him out of my school."

"Hmm," said Curio. "But Miss, don't we want him near the portal? If it opens suddenly we want him nearby so we can shove him through it."

"How on earth are we going to shove him through it?" asked Nikki. "He'd overpower both of us in a split second."

"We could hit him on the head with something," said Curio, making a ruthless bashing motion with his scrawny arms.

"That kind of thing could go horribly wrong," said Nikki. "We could miss and then he'd hit *us* on the head." She dug at the grass with the toe of her shoe. "Maybe we should try a different tactic. I was thinking maybe we could camp out each night right next to the portal, so we'll be on the spot if it opens again. Then you could go through and have Fuzz and Athena organize a bunch of castle guards to come here and drag Rufius back to the Realm of Reason."

"But Miss," said Curio, "we could be camping out next to the portal for days or even weeks. Somebody would notice us long before the portal opened. There ain't a lot of places to hide in that closet."

"Yeah, you're right," said Nikki. "It wasn't a great idea. I'm just feeling the need to do *something.* Maybe we could get Rufius arrested. If he was in jail it'd be a lot harder for him to cause any harm."

"Arrested?" asked Curio. "You mean the Rounders would throw him in the nearest dungeon?"

"Kind of," said Nikki. "Though we call them police here. And we don't have dungeons, which is unfortunate. If anyone deserves a dungeon it's Rufius. The problem is our legal system is really slow. That's mostly a good thing. The police have to collect lots of evidence and there's a trial before a jury and all that stuff. The slowness is supposed to prevent innocent people from getting thrown in jail. But it also keeps guilty people out of jail. Even if they've been accused of a crime they usually get bail, which means they pay money to the court and they stay free until after their trial." She sighed. "Nope. I don't think the whole arrest idea is going to help us. We're going to have to handle the Rufius problem on our own."

"Maybe we could pay a couple of big guys to beat him up," said Curio.

"Curio!" gasped Nikki. That's terrible. You're a better person than that."

"Sorry, Miss," said Curio. "I just really wants to see Rufius all laid out on the ground. Then I could kick him and kick him." He swung his walking boot in a ferocious kick and nearly toppled off the bench.

"Well, we're not going to hire someone to beat him up," said Nikki. "Just because he's a nasty sniveler doesn't mean we're going to lower ourselves to his level." Suddenly she let out a gasp and jumped off the bench.

"What is it, Miss?" asked Curio.

"Adulteration," said Nikki. "Or maybe just a complete substitution."

"Huh?" said Curio.

"Never mind," said Nikki. "It's just an idea that came to me all of a sudden. I need to look up some stuff in the reference books in the school chem lab. I'll meet you later at home. And I'll bring you some dinner."

# Chapter Five

## Harm Reduction

NIKKI WALKED ACROSS the empty soccer field. It was her free period, so she had no class to rush back to after lunch. As she entered the school through a side door near the gymnasium something Fortuna had said came back to her. Something about pushing through a wall. The chem lab could wait for a minute. She changed direction and headed for the portal closet.

Unfortunately when she got there the closet was in use. Banging sounds were coming from the half-open door. And this time it wasn't a sheep from the Realm of Reason. Not unless the sheep knew the lyrics to Hank William's 'Hey, Good Lookin' and could sing them in a wildly off-key voice. Nikki pulled out her phone, leaned against a locker, and tried to look inconspicuous.

After ten more minutes of banging someone emerged from the closet. It was Jerry. The oldest and crankiest of the school's janitors. He was pushing a cart containing a mop and a soapy bucket of water. He dunked the mop in the water and began to clean the linoleum floor. Very, very slowly.

Nikki edged out of the way as the mop inched toward her, but Jerry never even looked at her. After what seemed like an hour he and his mop sloshed their way around the corner and disappeared. Nikki glanced up and down the hallway. No one in sight. She darted into the closet and quietly shut the door. Given that Jerry's work speed was in the turtle and snail category it was unlikely he'd be back for a while. She headed to the back of the closet and opened the door to the old coal boiler. Fortuna had said she'd just put her hand on the wall of the alleyway in Cogent Town and the rest of her had suddenly melted through the wall. Nikki put the flat of her palm on the grimy metal inside the boiler and held it there. Nothing. No melting. All she felt was coal dust. She checked the time on her phone and left her hand on the wall of the boiler for ten minutes, but nothing happened. She sighed. Obviously, just touching the portal wasn't enough. She tucked her phone back in her pocket and was about to close the boiler door when suddenly she spotted a tiny movement in the boiler's dark interior. She pulled her phone back out and turned on its flashlight. The beam showed a tiny paw emerging from the grimy iron wall. It was a cat's paw. It flicked back and forth like it was trying to catch a butterfly. Nikki gently touched the paw with one finger. The paw instantly retreated back through the iron wall. There was a long pause, and then suddenly a cat shimmered into being, oozing through the iron wall of the boiler like melted butter.

"Cation!" Nikki gasped.

The cat launched itself out of the boiler and landed on Nikki's shoulder, purring loudly and rubbing her whiskers against Nikki's cheek.

"You're supposed to be up at Castle Cogent keeping their mouse population under control," said Nikki. "What were you doing in an alleyway down in Cogent Town?"

Nikki petted the cat with one hand and cautiously put her other hand back on the interior wall of the boiler. It felt just as cold, grimy, and solid as before. Neither her hand nor the rest of her melted through into the Realm of Reason.

"What do you think, Cation?" asked Nikki, untangling one of the cat's paws from her long dark hair. "Does the portal only work in one direction now? I went through it to the Realm a year ago. But I was with Fuzz and Athena. Maybe a person from the Realm has to be with me? I can't go through on my own?"

Cation just yawned and started kneading a hole through Nikki's T-shirt.

Nikki scooped up the cat and tucked her down at the bottom of her backpack. Cation growled at first, but after a bit of wriggling around she resigned herself to her fate and curled into a ball next to Nikki's chemistry textbook.

"Now you behave yourself in there," said Nikki, zipping up the backpack but leaving a gap so air could get in. "I don't have time to take you home right now. I've got one more class today." She checked the time. Half an hour left before her history class. She closed the boiler, shouldered her backpack, and went to the closet door. Before opening it she stood on her tiptoes and peered out of its tiny glass window. No one in sight. She eased the door open and slipped out into the hallway.

"Well, hello there."

Nikki staggered backwards, flattening herself against the closet door.

Rufius was leaning against a bank of lockers just down the hall from the closet. "I thought I heard someone talking in there," he said. "It sounded like a girl's voice, which was odd. All the cleaners in this place are men. I should know. I was one of them until yesterday." He smoothed the lapel of his purple jacket. "This costume suits me much better, don't you think?" He sauntered over to Nikki. "So, have you found out how to control the portal yet? An enterprising young lady such as yourself should have it all figured out by now."

"If I did know how to control it I'd shove you through it," said Nikki. "And then I'd lock it so you could never get back here."

Rufius grinned, but his black eyes stayed cold and hard. "You were quite a thorn in my side back in the Realm," he said. "But you had those blasted imps to help you over there. Here it's a different story."

"Yes, it is," said Nikki. "This is my world and you're just a visitor. You don't know how things work here."

"Oh, this world isn't all that hard to figure out," said Rufius. "I'll admit, some things were startling at first. I still don't understand how your buildings are lit at night, or what those metal things which travel very fast are. But I've acquired the basics. A place to sleep, food, and money. And speaking of money, I could use some more. I only managed to bring one bag of coins with me from the Realm when I came through the portal. I want to get more. I have quite a large haul of coins stashed away in a house in Cogent Town. That's where you come in. You're going to figure out how I can travel back and forth through the portal whenever I want."

Nikki snorted. "You think I'm going to *help* you? I'd rather push you off a cliff."

Rufius's dark eyes flashed dangerously and he took a step closer to her, but just then Jerry the janitor trudged into view pushing his mop.

"Hey!" Jerry shouted. "Get away from my closet! That's for janitors only. Not students or fancy-pants guidance counselors." He lumbered toward them, waving his mop.

Nikki ducked under the mop and took off down the hall at top speed. Her backpack started hissing, yowling and growling all at once. She ran past the cafeteria, dodged around a pack of boys playing hacky-sack, and skidded to a halt in front of the chemistry lab. There was no chem class scheduled, and sure enough, the lab was empty. She shut the door and locked it. Footsteps passed by, but no one tried to enter the lab.

"Yes, yes, I know you want out," she said to her backpack, setting it down on a lab bench. A paw pushed out of the opening in the zipper and waved back and forth furiously. Nikki unzipped the pack and Cation leaped out onto the worktop, nearly impaling herself on a microscope.

"Stay out of trouble," Nikki said, giving the cat a quick scratch under the chin. "I've got some work to do, and then I'll take you home. I'll make up some excuse for missing history class."

She went to the glass-fronted bookcase at the back of the classroom and pulled out the Oxford Dictionary of Chemistry. What she wanted was a way to neutralize phenylacetone without making it obvious that it had been tampered with. She doubted that the boys Rufius had been talking to in her chem class were stupid enough to actually try meth themselves. If they succeeded in making it they would try to sell it without testing it. Or Rufius would try to sell it. If she could make the meth harmless then their buyers would go elsewhere. And any Westlake High students they sold their stuff to wouldn't get hooked.

After an hour of wading through the Dictionary and several other reference books of organic chemistry she concluded that trying to interfere at the phenylacetone stage of the process wasn't going to work. If the phenylacetone was tampered with then the reactions further along in the process wouldn't happen and someone would notice. Her best bet was to try substitution rather than tampering. Simply replace the finished meth with a harmless substitute. She put the reference books back in the bookcase and pulled out her phone. A google search told her that powder was the most common form of meth, and that it looked similar to crystallized sugar and usually smelled faintly of ammonia or cat urine.

Nikki looked down at Cation, who was winding herself around her leg. "So, do you want to make a little contribution to this endeavor? It's for a good cause."

Cation meowed and started climbing up Nikki's jeans.

"Ouch!" said Nikki. She detached Cation's claws and tucked the cat back in her backpack. She left the chem lab and managed to leave the school grounds without running into any hall monitors, her history teacher, or Rufius. On the way home she stopped at a corner store and bought a ham sandwich for Curio and three cans of Fancy Feast, tuna flavor. Between Curio and now Cation her allowance money was starting to run low. If any more denizens of the Realm of Reason came through the portal she'd have to get a part-time job.

As she neared her apartment building she took a quick look up and down the block. No one in sight. She took off her backpack and shoved it through the hole under the yew hedge. The backpack yowled.

"Shhhh!" hissed Nikki as she crawled under the hedge. She put the pack back on and grabbed an ivy branch which looked like it was thick enough to support a girl, a cat, two textbooks and three cans of Fancy Feast. Climbing up the ivy turned out to be a lot harder than climbing down. Her chin and knuckles were scraped and sore by the time she reached the window. She made a mental note to find a rope to help Curio with the climb. She was about to tap on the window when it flew open.

"Oh, Miss," said Curio, leaning over the window ledge, "I'm happier than a pig in a puddle that you're here. We has company."

Nikki hauled herself over the windowsill and put her backpack on the floor. Cation immediately squeezed her way out. "Has Rufius found out where I live?" she asked.

"No, Miss," said Curio. "It ain't that bad, but it ain't great." He gestured for Nikki to follow him into the bedroom.

Nikki heard the snores before she saw the bedroom's occupant. She came to an abrupt halt in the doorway. There, tucked into her mom's sleeping bag, was Bertie. Also known as the King of the Realm of Reason.

"What the . . ." said Nikki, staring down at Bertie. She'd been hoping that Fuzz or Athena had come through the portal, or even the Prince of Physics. But she'd never expected Bertie of all people.

"How did he get here?" she stammered. "I mean here in my

building."

"I spotted him wandering around that big field behind your place of learning," said Curio. "So I brought him here. I didn't know what else to do with him. He was jumpy as a rabbit and kept saying that he wanted to go home. He meant back to the Realm. I tried to tell him that we don't have no control over the portal. That we couldn't just send him back. But he kept ordering me to open it. I finally threatened to leave him in the field. That seemed to spook him and he quieted down and let me bring him here. He says he wants pancakes with butter and honey for breakfast. And a bottle of your best brandy. I would recommend against that last item, Miss. Mr. Bertie, I mean his Highness, is a handful even when he's not drunk as a skunk. Miss Athena has been having a terrible time with him. He says he hates being King and that it's too much work and the crown makes his head hurt."

"So he went through the portal just to get away from Athena?" asked Nikki.

Curio shrugged.

Cation wandered in and sniffed at Bertie. She didn't seem to like what she smelled and started to squat next to his unshaven chin.

"No!" gasped Nikki. "Not there!" She grabbed the cat and dashed into the kitchen, dumping her in the sink. "*Now* you can let loose."

Cation meowed in satisfaction as she left a small brown present next to the garbage disposal.

"A litter box," said Nikki with a sigh. "Another hit to my allowance." She plopped Cation on the floor and washed the smelly deposit down the drain.

"Is this your kitty from the Realm, Miss?" asked Curio, rubbing Cation's ears.

"Yeah," said Nikki. "She came through the portal an hour ago. So far that makes four people, one sheep, and a cat."

"Huh," said Curio. "I wonder why it's kind of easy to get here but so hard to get back. I tried and tried, but no luck."

"Maybe we could try sending a message through." said Nikki. "A note saying 'please send Rounders or castle guards. Rufius is here and causing trouble.' Though if no one was in the alleyway in Cogent Town our note would probably just get blown away by the wind."

"I don't know as a note would be much help, Miss," said Curio. "Mr. Fuzz and Miss Athena already know that Rufius is here. I'm sure they're already trying everything they can to get help to you."

"Yeah, that's true," said Nikki. "Well, in the meantime we'll just have to manage on our own. I have an idea about how to stop Rufius's latest plot, or at least to slow it down a bit. Cation is going to help."

Cation wrapped herself around Nikki's legs, purring loudly.

Nikki glanced at the bedroom. "You can't stay here tonight. Without the sleeping bag you'll freeze. I guess I'll have to sneak you into my room. You can sleep on the floor. It's got a thick carpet and I've got plenty of extra blankets. My mom's pretty good about knocking. You should have time to hide in the closet if she wants to come in."

"What about your kitty, Miss?" asked Curio.

"She'll have to stay here," said Nikki. "I'll clean up any messes she makes tomorrow. C'mon. Let's go upstairs. My mom might not be home from work yet. That'll make things easier."

# Chapter Six

## Babysitting

"CURIO" WHISPERED NIKKI. "Wake up."

Curio groaned and burrowed deeper into the pile of blankets on the floor of Nikki's room.

Nikki tickled the tiny foot which was sticking out of the pile. The blankets stirred and one by one peeled away until Curio was revealed, wearing an old nightgown of Nikki's with pink tulips on it. His blond hair stuck up as if he'd been electrocuted.

"I'm up, Miss," he yawned. "Awfully early, ain't it?" He looked out the window, where the sunrise was just barely poking through the curtains. "I thought you said you don't have no school today."

"I don't," said Nikki. "It's Saturday. But I just heard my mom talking on the phone with old Mrs. Evanston from downstairs. I didn't catch the whole conversation, but it sounded like Mrs. Evanston was complaining about a strange man banging on her front door. He was yelling about being a King and wanting pancakes. Rocky tried to bite his ankles and he ran off toward the lake. Get dressed quick. We need to find him."

"Right, Miss," said Curio. He grabbed his T-shirt and jeans and ducked into the closet.

Nikki carefully opened the door of her bedroom. The apartment was quiet and dark. She closed the door again. "I think my mom's gone back to sleep," she said. "I thought she might have called the police, but I guess she didn't think there was any danger. She probably thought Mrs. Evanston meant that the strange man was banging on the lobby door. That happens sometimes. It's usually just someone with the wrong address. My mom must not have realized that Bertie was actually inside the building."

"He almost wasn't, Miss," said Curio, opening the closet door and sitting on the floor to pull on his walking boot. "I had an awful time getting him to climb the ivy on your building. He laid down on the grass and refused to budge. I finally threatened to leave him there all night. That did the trick. Mr. Bertie's as bad as Rufius at roughing it. It's strictly feather beds and downy pillows for those two."

"Put your baseball cap on," said Nikki. "And put your coat on. It's cold outside."

Curio pulled on the old parka that Nikki had found in the back of her closet. She'd worn it until age twelve. It had holes in the elbows and mysterious stains, but it was double-lined and warm.

Nikki picked up the milk carton she'd given Curio to use as a chamber pot and dumped the contents out the window. "Wait here while I change." She shut herself in the closet and quickly pulled on jeans and a heavy sweater topped with a wind-breaker. "Put your blankets back in there," she said as she emerged, pointing at an old toy chest now used for storage. "I'm going to see if the coast is clear."

She eased open the bedroom door and tiptoed down the hall in stocking feet. A very faint sound of slow breathing came from her mother's bedroom. She tiptoed back, grabbed her backpack and her Nikes off the floor, and motioned to Curio to follow her. They made no sound as they crept along the carpeted hallway, but the small entranceway near the front door was covered in creaky polished wood. Nikki waved Curio to a halt and flattened herself against the wall. By keeping her feet at the very edge of the floor she managed to inch along without a sound. She eased open the front door and motioned to Curio. Edging the wall was harder for Curio due to his walking boot, but he managed. Nikki closed the front door behind them and hurriedly shoved on her Nikes.

As they passed the second-floor apartment they could hear Cation mewling plaintively.

"Should we let your kitty out, Miss?" Curio whispered.

"No," said Nikki. "I'll feed her when we get back. And we'll have to do some cleaning. My guess is she's sprayed in every corner."

They crept past the ground floor apartment, earning just a faint growl from Rocky. The morning sun was just brightening the faded yellow roses in the front garden as they emerged from the building. Nikki came to a halt on the front sidewalk, unsure where to go. Suddenly Curio tugged on her arm.

"Miss, look!" he said, pointing at something shiny on the sidewalk.

Nikki bent down and picked it up. "It's a gold coin," she said. "A Realm coin. Bertie must have brought some with him, just like Rufius did."

"Here's another one!" said Curio, wandering down the sidewalk. "And another one. They seems to be headed that way, to the lake. Do you think Mr. Bertie's dropping them on purpose?"

"I doubt it," said Nikki. "It's an awfully expensive trail of bread-crumbs."

They followed the trail of dropped coins down to the lake, Nikki tucking each one into the pocket of her jeans. They were quite heavy, and by the time they reached the lake she was listing to one side. The golden trail led them along the lakeshore toward the white dome of the state capital. As they passed a little swimming beach Nikki spotted a man sitting on the sand. She squinted at him, decided it wasn't Bertie, and was about to go on when Curio suddenly headed straight for the man.

Nikki followed him across the sand, and as she got closer she realized that Curio was right. Bertie was sitting hunched over, his head buried in his hands. He was dressed in the plain, homemade clothes of a Realm farmer, which was why she hadn't recognized him. The Bertie she knew from the Realm, the nephew of the King, was fond of brightly colored silk tunics, velvet cloaks, and feathered caps, giving him the appearance of a human peacock. Dressed in a farmer's rough wool tunic and trousers he was nearly unrecognizable.

"Hello Mr. Bertie," said Curio. "I mean Your Highness. Sir. How's it going?"

A long sigh escaped from Bertie. "It's not going well. I never should have come here. I don't know what I was thinking. I *wasn't* thinking. That's always been my problem. I'm just not good at thinking. My own father used to tell me so. And now Athena wants me to think all the time. I have to think about the agricultural output of the Realm. I have to think about our trade relations with the Southern Isles. I have to think about how many pig farms there are near Kingston. What do I know about pigs? Nothing. I like a nice rasher of bacon as much as the next person, but how that bacon is produced is not a subject I wish to know in more detail."

He picked up a pebble and threw it in a very un-athletic manner into the lake. "It was just too much. All of Athena's demands, all the nobles and courtiers constantly insisting they needed new titles and more land. I even had to spend two hours every day sitting in the throne room listening to the complaints of ordinary citizens. You don't know the meaning of the word dull until you've had to listen to a Cogent Town shoemaker complain that the local tannery is charging him too much for leather."

He sighed again. "I thought going through the portal would be an escape from all the drudgery of being King, but now that I'm here in this very strange world I just want to go back home. I'll go back and tell Athena that she'll just have to find someone else to be King. I'm not fit for the job." He stood up and brushed the sand off his trousers. "Yes, that's the ticket. I should have resigned weeks ago. I just couldn't bear to hurt Athena's feelings. She's always been fond of me. But it has to be done. Things can't go on as they are, with me trying to cram pig facts into my head. I try to keep the pigs in my head, but they just run right back out again. Come on young Curio, let's go back through the portal right now. I'm sure you're missing your homeland just as much as I am. This strange place is too gruesome for words. Those metal carriages have nearly flattened me on numerous occasions. I'll not survive another day here."

"But Mr. Bertie," said Curio. "We can't go back. Likes I already told you, I tried to go back, with no luck. The portal just ain't working from this side."

"But surely this young lady knows how to make it work," said Bertie, making a kingly bow to Nikki. "I watched her do great deeds in the fight to save Cogent Town from those unspeakable ruffians. Such a person must have many brilliant ideas as to how to open the portal and send me home."

"Sorry, but no," said Nikki. "I don't know how the portal works any more than Curio does. All we know is that it seems to be easier to travel from the Realm to here than the other way around. You might be stuck here for a while."

Bertie whimpered and collapsed back into a hunched heap on the sand.

"What are we gonna do with him, Miss?" Curio whispered over Bertie's head.

Nikki tugged on her hair in frustration. "I don't know. We can't just leave him here. The police might pick him up as a vagrant. And if he starts telling them he's a King in another world they'll think he's crazy and take him to the mental hospital."

"Should we try to get him back to your house?" asked Curio.

Nikki shook her head. "He's too noisy to stay there. My mom'll notice right away that there's someone in the empty apartment. Then she'll call the police and we'll be in the same pickle, trying to get

Bertie out of the mental hospital." She pulled a handful of the Realm coins out of her pocket and held them in front of Bertie. "You've been dropping these," she said, shaking them. "Do you have more of them?"

Bertie nodded dejectedly. "I brought a whole bag of them from the Realm. I thought I could buy a nice little country estate here. Some place to relax and not have to think about pigs ever again. But I didn't realize this world would be so unpleasant. And it's definitely not relaxing."

Nikki looked around on the sand but didn't see a bag of coins. "What did you do with the rest?" she asked.

"I dropped them down there," said Bertie, gesturing vaguely along the beach. "They were too heavy and I couldn't carry them any farther."

Nikki and Curio headed down the beach in the direction they'd come. It took them quite a while to find the bag, which was a burlap sack the exact same color as the sand. Neither of them could lift it. Nikki tried dragging it, but she only managed to move it a few feet. She gave up and looked around for ideas. A small rowboat tied to a nearby dock caught her eye.

Curio noticed where she was looking. "Oh, Miss," he said. "I dunno know abouts that. Will we get in awful trouble?"

"We might get in trouble," said Nikki. "But I doubt it'll be awful trouble. It's handy being a kid sometimes, and stealing a rowboat is in the category of 'kids just goofing off'. And besides, there's no one around. We should be able to return it before anyone even notices."

Nikki thought they'd have trouble getting Bertie to cooperate, but he seemed so glad to have someone telling him what to do that he eagerly retrieved the bag of coins and got into the rowboat with it. Curio climbed in and perched in the bow. Nikki untied the boat from the dock and grabbed the oars. Her first thought was to head for home. But as she slowly rowed in that direction, trying to decide what to do, she suddenly had a better idea about how to solve the Bertie problem. She gave a strong pull on the left oar and swung the rowboat in the other direction, toward the white dome of the state house.

"Miss, what are you doing?" asked Curio. "This is the wrong way."

"We can't take Bertie home," said Nikki. "Like I said, he's just too noisy. But I've just thought of another place he could stay. The YMCA. It's kind of like an Inn for people who can't pay much. It's up there, not far from that big white building with the dome. The Y isn't free, but we can use the bag of coins to pay for it. They should last for quite a long time. I'll take a few over to that antique shop where Rufius traded his coins for dollars. You wait in the boat with Bertie."

It took a bit of doing, but they managed to get Bertie successfully installed at the Madison YMCA. They hid the bag of coins in an alley next to the Y, under a pile of rotting cardboard boxes, and Nikki paid the clerk at the front desk enough to hold Bertie's room for a week. Curio went upstairs with him to show him how to use the communal showers and toilets.

"I don't know, Miss," said Curio as they waved goodbye to a forlorn Bertie and headed down the steps of the Y. "What if Mr. Bertie runs around that place telling everyone he's a king? I don't think that'll go down so well."

"It'll be okay," said Nikki. "I told the desk clerk that Bertie has some mental issues. Some days he thinks he's a king, some days he thinks he's a giraffe. The Y is used to people like that. The desk clerk said it's not a problem as long as Bertie isn't violent."

Curio laughed. "Mr. Bertie's about as violent as a baby bunny asleep in a bunch of daffydillys. Mind you, he's not a coward. He does seem kinda timid-like, but you should've seen how he helped track down all the Knights of the Iron Fist who tried to overthrow the King. I don't think he's really all that fond of his uncle, our old King. But he's powerful fond of Miss Athena. And it was one of the Knights of the Iron Fist who shot her in the leg with an arrow during the invasion of ImpHaven."

"How's she doing?" asked Nikki. "Has she recovered?"

"Kinda," said Curio. "She has to use a crutch to get around, and her leg pains her though she won't admit it."

Nikki sighed. "I'm sorry. Let's hope she comes through the portal. Our medical knowledge is much more advanced than yours. Our doctors could probably help her."

Nikki turned into the alley where they'd left the bag of coins and pulled the cardboard boxes off it. "Maybe if we split it up?" she said. "Try putting a handful in each pocket of your jeans."

Curio crammed as many coins as he could into his pockets and took a step. He crumpled to the ground.

"Sorry," said Nikki, helping him up. "Obviously that's not gonna work. We need some kind of transport, and I hear a possibility." She pointed to the end of the alley, where loud screams were coming over a brick wall.

"Sounds like a bunch of kids being punished," said Curio. "Do you have floggings here, Miss?"

Nikki laughed. "No. It's just kids playing. It must be a school or a daycare center. Come on."

They waited by the wall until the kids were called inside and the noise stopped. Nikki pulled a trash can against the wall and stood on top of it to see over. "I see something that might work," she whispered. "Wait here."

She scrambled over the wall and grabbed the pink Big Wheel she'd spotted. "Curio," she hissed, "can you reach it? I need both hands free to climb back over."

Curio's baseball cap appeared over the wall. He grabbed the front wheel of the tricycle Nikki was holding up and yanked it over.

Nikki scrambled back over and wheeled the trike up to the bag of coins. With Curio's help she managed to drag the bag onto the seat of the Big Wheel. The plastic seat sagged nearly to the ground, but it didn't break.

Their walk back to the lake was slow and awkward, with Nikki bent nearly double trying to guide the tricycle's tiny handlebars, but they finally reached the dock where they'd left the rowboat. Nikki tied an extra knot into the neck of the burlap bag of coins and then shoved the Big Wheel off the dock, coins and all, into the boat. She grabbed the oars and Curio hopped into his perch on the bow.

"Ain't we gonna return that little pink cart, Miss?" he asked as Nikki rowed toward home.

"I'll do it later," said Nikki. "We'll need it to get the bag from the dock to my building."

AN HOUR LATER they crawled through the hole in the yew hedge surrounding Nikki's building and collapsed on the grass in the side yard. Both the rowboat and the Big Wheel had been returned, and the bag of coins was safely buried under a dark corner of the yew hedge where only squirrels and the occasional robin ventured. Nikki had stuffed a handful of the coins into the pockets of her jeans, enough to pay for several weeks at the Y for Bertie.

"I have something I need to do today," Nikki finally said, getting up from the grass and brushing off her jeans. "I guess you could hang out here in the yard if you want. No one can see you, and no one ever comes out here. I'll get you some books to read when I come back, to make it less boring for you here. I'd loan you the little TV I have in my bedroom, but my mom would hear the noise when she passes your apartment on the stairs."

"What's a TV, Miss?" asked Curio.

"It's a kind of device we use for entertainment," Nikki said. "It's sort of like watching a play."

Curio just blinked at her. "You have a troop of players in your room, Miss? I didn't see any."

"No, no," said Nikki. "The people on the TV aren't real. They're sort of like people in a painting, except they move and talk."

Now Curio looked alarmed, as if he was worried that Nikki had suddenly lost her mind.

Nikki would have found his expression funny, except she knew that more of these frustrating conversations were going to come up in the future. The longer Curio stayed in Madison the more necessary it would be to explain modern life to him.

"Can I go for a walk, Miss?" asked Curio.

"I guess so," said Nikki. "Just keep your baseball cap on. But, we just did a lot of walking. Doesn't your foot hurt?"

"A little bit," said Curio. "But this strange boot you got me helps a lot."

"That's good," said Nikki. "But still, don't overdo it. Having to take you to a doctor would be really hard. They'd ask us all kinds of questions, and want to know why our parents weren't with us. They might even refuse to treat you without an adult present."

"Okay, Miss," said Curio. "I was just gonna walk down to the lake. I likes looking at the water and the sailboats. It's too bad I didn't take Daisy through the portal with me. She was a big help when my foot got too sore for walking. Though she could be an ornery little monster when she wanted to be. She dumped me right in a mud puddle once. I had to feed her an entire blueberry pie before she let me ride her again."

Nikki laughed. "It's probably a good thing you didn't bring her. You need to keep a low profile, and riding a donkey around downtown Madison would probably get you on the evening news. Tell you what, when I get back I'll teach you how to ride my bike. I think I can lower the seat and handlebars enough for you."

"What's a bike, Miss?" asked Curio.

"I'll explain later," said Nikki. "I need to get going. I should be back by dinnertime. In the meantime, stay out of trouble."

# Chapter Seven

## A Wrench in the Works

NIKKI SQUINTED THROUGH a crack in the clapboard wall of the old one-car garage. The garage looked like it hadn't been used in years. The prairie grass surrounding it hadn't been mowed in so long that it came up to her waist. All Nikki could see through the crack was a paint can with faded letters and an open lid. She stood up and checked the area carefully again. No people in sight, and no sound except the chittering of a couple of squirrels as they chased each other through the grass. The field was surrounded on all sides by a thick forest of Jack pines. The only sign of recent activity was a patch of flattened weeds near the garage's side door.

Nikki waded through the grass to the side door and tried the handle. Locked. She was tempted to have a go at it with the screwdriver she'd put in her backpack, but she didn't want to leave any noticeable marks. She put her nose to the door jamb and sniffed. All she smelled was motor oil and rotting wood. No hint of cat urine or ammonia to indicate that this was a meth lab.

The garage was on a farm owned by the Dinsfeld family. Bobby Dinsfeld was one of the boys who'd been talking with Rufius in her chemistry class. The other boy lived in an apartment building, so she'd not bothered going there. The isolated Dinsfeld farm was a much more promising location for nefarious activities. She'd known where Bobby lived. They'd both gone on a class field trip once, and the school bus had dropped him off at the edge of the farm.

Giving up on the side door she waded through the grass to the back of the garage. Rusty farm equipment was stacked against it, including a huge threshing machine that looked like something belonging to the Jawas in Star Wars. Nikki half-expected R2-D2 to roll out of it. It was an old John Deere thresher from the 1930's. It would have been pulled by a tractor, so it had no cabin for the operator. Nikki climbed up the rusty feeding chute and peered over the top. The grain pan was empty except for an abandoned bird's nest. She was about to climb down again when she suddenly froze, one foot swinging in mid-air. A car was approaching, from the pine forest. There must be a dirt road nearby that she hadn't seen on her trip up to the farm. After the city bus had dropped her off she'd had a long trek through the woods, keeping to the trees to avoid being seen by anyone in the farmhouse off in the distance. She hadn't seen any sign of car tracks in the woods and the driveway up to the garage had long ago been covered up by grass.

She quickly climbed up to the top of the thresher and lowered herself into the grain pan. It was half-covered on top by a metal grate. She edged under the grate and sat down, trying to hear the car above the beating of her heart. The car engine died and she heard doors slam. A boy's voice said something she couldn't quite hear and footsteps crackled through the forest undergrowth. She was so intent on the voices that at first she barely noticed the pressure on her arm. She brushed at her arm without looking, thinking it was just an old stalk of wheat leftover from the machine's final harvest. But then the pressure started to wrap around her arm. She looked down and bit her tongue so hard to keep from screaming that she drew blood. A snake had wrapped itself around her bicep and was twisting itself down toward her wrist. In the semi-darkness she couldn't see the snake's markings clearly. She frantically tried to think. Poisonous snakes were rare in Wisconsin. The only one she could think of was the timber rattlesnake. She squinted at the snake. It looked like it had the brown horizontal stripes of a rattlesnake, but it was heavy, and it felt too thick for a rattler. A bull snake, she decided, hoping that wasn't just wishful thinking. Bull snakes weren't poisonous, but they did bite when threatened. She kept as still as possible, her outstretched arm shaking slightly as the heavy snake wound slowly along it. After what seemed like hours she felt the weight on her arm lessen. The snake slithered off her and dropped down through a rusty hole in the grain pan.

Her whole body shuddered with relief and she wiped cold sweat off her forehead. It took a while to turn her attention back to listening. She couldn't hear the voices anymore, but rattling and banging noises were coming from inside the old garage. The minutes stretched into hours and the light coming in through cracks in the rusty metal sides of the thresher turned dim. Finally she heard the side door of the garage creak open.

"So, are you done?"

It was Rufius.

"Not yet. Give us another couple of days. This ain't easy."

A boy's voice. Probably Bobby Dinsfeld, Nikki thought. It was a deep voice, just on the edge of adulthood, and Bobby was bigger and older than the other boy Rufius had talked with in her chem class.

"Why can't we just sell the first batch?" asked Rufius.

"Dude, I already told you. The first batch was crap. A mouse couldn't get high on it."

Nikki was surprised by the impatience in Bobby's voice. He obviously wasn't afraid of Rufius. Maybe it was because he was big for a teenager, or maybe he wasn't aware of what Rufius was capable of. Bobby's remark about the mouse was worrisome. It implied that Bobby had tried the first batch himself. Nikki was really surprised. She'd expected the boys to focus on selling the meth, not on using it.

If they were going to try each batch then her plan to substitute sugar for their final product wasn't going to work.

"Fine," snapped Rufius. "Come see me in my office when it's ready."

Nikki heard the door of the garage close, and a quiet swishing noise floated through the evening air as they waded through the grass back to the forest. She huddled in the thresher for a long time after they'd left, unable to tell for certain whether anyone had stayed behind. She stayed in her hiding place until it was dark out and an owl started to hoot from somewhere in the forest. She climbed noiselessly out and peered around the side of the garage. No one was near the side door and no light showed from inside. She gave the door handle a quick try but it was still locked.

The moon hadn't risen yet. It was so dark that it was impossible for anyone in the distant farmhouse to see her. She didn't bother going back through the woods. She headed into the grass, making a beeline for the road and the bus stop.

"THIS ISN'T WORKING," said Nikki, wrinkling her nose at the smell of cat pee coming from every corner of the empty apartment. She'd returned from her trip to the Dinsfeld farm to find that Cation had marked her territory with a vengeance. "Who knew that such a small cat could pee so much. Keep blotting the puddles with toilet paper. I'll be right back." She left Curio in the apartment and ran upstairs.

She returned a minute later with a roll of paper towels and a spray bottle of Windex. "This stuff isn't going to smell much better than cat pee, but hopefully it will at least kill the germs." She handed Curio the paper towels. "I'll spray, you wipe."

Cation watched their attempt to clean up her messes with intense interest. After she tried to drink the blue stream of liquid coming out of the Windex bottle Nikki picked her up and shut her in the cupboard under the kitchen sink. The litterbox that Nikki had bought on her way home from the Dinsfeld farm sat unused in a corner by the fridge.

"I have to get upstairs to dinner," said Nikki after the last puddle was sprayed and wiped up. "Otherwise my mom'll come looking for me. See if you can get Cation to start using the litterbox."

"I'll lure her into it with pieces of this chicken," said Curio, tearing open the plastic package of sliced chicken Nikki had brought him and shoving a piece in his mouth. "That should do the trick."

"Geez, Curio," said Nikki. "What did I tell you about washing your hands? You've got cat-pee germs all over them."

Curio peered closely at his hands, as if expecting them to erupt in purple spots. "I don't see none of these germ things you keep talking about, Miss," he said. "Maybe they've fallen off?" He looked around on the floor.

"They're on your hands even though you can't see them," said Nikki. "Germs are tiny little micro-organisms too small for us to see. They come in different forms, like bacteria, viruses, and fungi. I have a microscope up in my room. One day when my mom isn't home I'll show you some bacteria under the microscope." She'd come to realize that Curio might have a long stay in Madison, and that her original plan to keep him ignorant of modern life wasn't going to work. He was going to have to learn a few things whether she liked it or not.

Curio disappeared into the bathroom and came back wiping his wet hands on his jeans. "Are we gonna keep your kitty cooped up here all the time, Miss?" he asked. "It don't seem quite fair."

"No," said Nikki. "I've been thinking about that. My mom is allergic to cats, so I can't bring Cation upstairs. But if I get some rope and a basket we can lower her out the window into the side yard every day, and haul her up at night. She won't stay in the yard, of course. She'll explore the neighborhood. She runs the risk of getting hit by a car, but it still seems kinder than keeping her locked up here."

Nikki collected all the used paper towels into a plastic garbage bag and shoved it under the kitchen sink. Cation dashed out as soon as the cupboard door opened. "So, are you all set for the night?"

Curio nodded. He went to the kitchen counter and picked up the paperback book and the flashlight that Nikki had brought him. "I gots my funny looking scroll and my candle-thing." He started flicking the flashlight on and off, aiming the beam all over the floor. Cation pounced on the spots of light and neither she nor Curio noticed when Nikki slipped quietly out of the apartment.

# Chapter Eight

## Anonymous

"YOU'RE STRAW-MANNING ME," snapped Tina, aiming her pencil at Nikki like a dart thrower eyeing her target.

"I am not," said Nikki, fighting the urge to duck under her desk. It wouldn't be the first time Tina had thrown a pencil at her in debate class. The last time it had barely missed her left eye.

"Yes, you are," said Mr. Tomlinson, snatching Tina's pencil out of her hand and placing it on his desk. "That's the move of a rank amateur, Murrow. The judges will spot it right away and drop your score. You'll need to do much better if our team is going to make it to the district championship this year. Today's topic is: should fast food be banned in high school cafeterias. Tina, arguing the negative, merely said that some students prefer fast food and student preferences should be taken into account. You, arguing the affirmative, then claimed she wants to ruin students' health. Classic Straw Man fallacy, mis-representing your opponent's argument. In a formal debate that would be a five-point drop in your score, at a minimum. If you continue like this I'm going to boot you off the team. Is that understood?"

Nikki nodded, feeling her cheeks turning red. She knew Mr. Tomlinson was right. She'd not been focusing on her schoolwork very well. Ever since Rufius had come through the portal her concentration had been shot to pieces. Still, she could do without Tina sniggering at her. She balled up a piece of notebook paper and threw it at Tina, hitting her in the nose.

"That's it, Murrow," barked Mr. Tomlinson. "I've had enough. Go see the guidance counselor. Maybe he can talk some sense into you." He handed her a hall pass and pointed at the door.

Cheeks burning, Nikki grabbed her backpack and snatched the piece of paper out of his hand. She was out the door before it dawned on her that she'd just been ordered to go see Rufius. She came to a stop in the empty hallway. There had to be a way out. There was no way she was going to be in a room alone with him. She stared down at the hall pass. It had a place at the bottom for a teacher's or school official's signature. She might be able to convince Mrs. Halley, the principal's assistant, to sign it. She could say she'd met with the guidance counselor but he'd forgotten to sign her pass. Mrs. Halley was a sweet elderly lady who brought home-made cupcakes every week and handed them out to any student unlucky enough to be sent to the principal. It was usually easy to convince her to do things. Probably too easy.

The guidance counselor was in the same cluster of offices as the principal. When Nikki arrived the reception area was empty. There was a plate of rainbow-frosted cupcakes on the counter, but no one was on duty. She could hear voices, however. Two men were arguing behind the closed door of Rufius's office. Rufius's voice she recognized right away. It was cold and controlled even in anger. The other man had a slight lisp and an odd accent. It took her a minute to realize that it was Bertie.

The office door suddenly slammed open and Bertie rushed out, his pale delicate face even whiter than usual. Before Nikki had a chance to duck back into the hallway Rufius appeared and they both stood staring at her.

"It's . . . I just . . ." stammered Bertie.

"We were just discussing a private piece of business," said Rufius calmly. "Nothing to concern yourself with."

Mrs. Halley came in at that moment, carrying a plate of cupcakes that wafted a warm vanilla fragrance across the tension in the room. She offered the plate to Bertie, who took a cupcake and held onto it as if he didn't know quite what to do with it. Rufius curtly shook his head at Mrs. Halley and disappeared back into his office. He didn't slam the door, but it shut with a distinctly 'do not disturb' sound.

"Would you like one, dear?" Mrs. Halley asked Nikki.

"Thank you," said Nikki, taking one. "Um, Mrs. Halley, would you please sign this for me?" She held out the hall pass.

"Of course, dear," said Mrs. Halley. She put the plate of cupcakes on the reception counter and peered around in her usual vague and helpless way. "I don't know what I did with my reading glasses. I've misplaced three pairs this week. My son says he's going to glue them to my head. He's teasing, of course, but he has a point. It gets expensive always losing things. I used to lose countless mittens and scarves every winter when I was a child. My parents started making me buy them myself, out of my allowance. And rightly so. Oh, well. Put your paper on the counter, my dear. And just put your finger where I need to sign. I'm afraid the result will be sloppy, but in my experience teachers never check these things."

Nikki thanked Mrs. Halley, tucked the hall pass in the pocket of her jeans, took a bite of the cupcake, and motioned Bertie to follow her. She led him through the deserted hallways and out the side door of the school to the soccer field. The cross-country team was doing a warm-up run along the edge of the field. She waited for them to pass and led Bertie to her lunchtime bench near the woods where the Realm sheep had disappeared.

They sat in silence, eating their cupcakes and watching the cross-country team do their laps.

Finally Nikki balled up the cupcake wrapper, tucked it into the side pocket of her backpack, and turned to look at Bertie.

Bertie's ears turned red and he stared fixedly at the ground.

"Bertie, you have to tell me what happened," said Nikki.

Bertie suddenly became fascinated by an ant crawling along the bench.

"Bertie!" snapped Nikki.

Bertie shrugged in an unconvincingly casual way. "Nothing happened. Not really. It's just that Rufius is staying in that same very uncomfortable place you left me in. We ran into each other in the dining room, if you can call it that, with its scarred tables and its broken chairs and its ridiculous little boxes of something they call cereal. Honestly, would it kill them to put down a few freshly pressed white linen tablecloths? I suggested as much to one of the staff and now he calls me My Lord every time I see him. I assure you it is *not* a sign of respect."

"Hmm," said Nikki. "Okay. Well, it's not great that Rufius is staying there, but it's not the end of the world. It might even be a good thing. You can keep an eye on him."

"Keep an eye on him!" gasped Bertie. "He's a dangerous criminal! He's wanted in the Realm for treason! For masterminding an armed revolt!"

"I know, I know," said Nikki. "But he's not wanted for treason here in Madison. My point is that he's trying to paint himself as a solid citizen. A hero who saved our school principal from drowning. A respectable young man who's got a good job as a guidance counselor. I doubt that you're in any immediate danger from him. If he attacks you he'll just mess up the picture he's trying to paint. And, look, I don't want to play the kid card, but you're a grown man. If Rufius were to attack you at least you'd have a fighting chance. If he were to go after me or Curio . . ."

Bertie waved his arms wildly around his head, as if fighting off Nikki's last comment the way he'd fight off a swarm of bees. His expressive face went from horrified to embarrassed and back to horrified in the space of three seconds. Instead of answering he retreated back into his obsession with the ant. He sprinkled cupcake crumbs on his leg and watched it crawl up his knee.

"Did Rufius ask you about the portal?" said Nikki. "About how to open it?"

Bertie nodded. "Yes, but I don't know how it works and he didn't seem surprised by my lack of expertise on the subject. No one ever seems surprised by my lack of expertise. My incompetence in all things is something of a legend in the Realm." He sighed. "That hasn't stopped Athena from trying to mold me into a paragon of efficiency. She had me spending hours in the Castle Cogent library with stacks of ledgers listing how many bushels of wheat and barley the Realm exports to other lands. Barley! Engaging in light banter at card parties. *That* is what I excel at. Dealing with sums and ledgers is for people who lack my finesse at gossiping while executing a delicate minuet across a parquet-floored ballroom under crystal chandeliers. I've *told* Athena this, many times, but the point never seems to sink in. She just plops another enormous ledger down in front of me and hands me a quill."

"Well," said Nikki, "a knowledge of accounting and record-keeping *is* a very important skill for a ruler to have. And agricultural exports are vital to your economy. You're King now. You have to learn to deal with these things."

"You sound just like Athena," grumped Bertie.

"That's because I admire her backbone and her work-ethic," said Nikki. "Though I admit, I don't always agree with her. She's very pro-monarchy and I'm firmly pro-democracy."

"What's democracy?" asked Bertie.

"Nope," said Nikki, shaking her head. "We're not getting side-tracked by politics. Back to the point. What is going on between you and Rufius? Why were you in his office?"

Bertie suddenly became entranced by the ant again. "Nothing is 'going on', as you put it," he said. "As I told you, we just happened to meet in that revolting dining room of the . . . what is that place called again?"

"The YMCA," said Nikki.

"Yes," said Bertie. "Ridiculous name. Anyway, after our mutual surprise we exchanged a few words and he left. I attempted to choke down a few mouthfuls of the slop they feed us and then went for a walk along the lake."

"That still doesn't explain how you ended up in his office," said Nikki. "Did you follow him?"

"Good gracious, no!" Bertie exclaimed. "My motto in life is if you avoid mad dogs you're less likely to get bitten."

"Bertie," said Nikki. "Curio and I are your only friends in this land. Do you want us to abandon you? Leave you to cope on your own?"

A cascade of terror ran down Bertie's face, leaving it ashen and gray. "All right, all right. When we met in the dining room of that YMCA place Rufius mentioned that he might know a way to open the portal so that we could go home. He asked me to come to his office in your place of learning to discuss it. I was lucky to arrive there alive. It was a long walk from the lake and I was nearly flattened many times by those iron Hell-Beasts."

"Rufius doesn't know how to open the portal any more than you or I do," said Nikki. "He must want something from you. Did he ask you for money? Did you give him any of your Realm coins?"

Bertie shook his head. "No, he didn't ask for money. In fact, I was surprised that he didn't. He was incredibly greedy for riches when he took power in the Realm. The people in the Royal Treasury are still trying to sort out the real gold coins from the fake ones he had made of tin covered in gold foil. Apparently Rufius's goal was to loot the entire treasury."

Nikki sighed and stood up, brushing off cupcake crumbs. She could tell that Bertie was hiding something, but it was clear that whatever it was he wasn't going to tell her. She'd ask Curio to try and wrangle it out of him.

"I don't suppose you could get me something to eat?" asked Bertie. "The staff at that place you left me in said they don't provide any food other than the morning meal."

"Sure," said Nikki. "It's almost lunchtime. I have an hour until my next class. I'll show you where the nearest Quik-Mart is. It's on the way back to the Y. You can get sandwiches, yogurt, basic stuff like that."

"Does this Quick Market take gold?" asked Bertie, digging in his pocket for Realm coins.

"No," said Nikki. "But I have enough dollars to buy you some lunch and probably enough for dinner as well. Tomorrow I'll take you to the pawn shop I've been using and show you how to exchange your gold for dollars. Fortunately the pawn shop owner hasn't asked too many questions about where I'm getting the gold coins from. Probably because he's making a profit each time I come in. He's been giving me twenty dollars for each gold coin, so don't let him cheat you and give you less. The coins are probably worth more than that, but I can't go to a more reputable dealer. They'd ask questions about where the coins came from and if my parents know I'm going to a pawnbroker."

She shouldered her backpack and led Bertie across the soccer field and off the high school grounds. They got a few stares as they walked through the streets of downtown, mostly because Bertie jumped every time a car passed him. When an ambulance passed them blaring its siren he plastered himself to the side of the nearest building.

Nikki peeled him off. "Look, Bertie, you're just going to have to get used to cars. I know they're loud and scary, but if you follow a few rules you'll be okay. See this long white strip of pavement we're standing on? It's called a sidewalk. Cars don't drive on the sidewalk, so as long as you stay on it you'll be okay. See that white light over there that says 'Walk'? That means it's okay to cross the street to the sidewalk on the other side. That red light hanging above the street means the cars have to stop to let you cross. See? We've got a walk signal. Let's cross. The Quik Mart is over there on the corner."

Like Curio Bertie was fascinated by the bright lights and refrigerated cases in the store. He stuck his head in the ice cream case for so long that Nikki spotted the store clerk frowning at them. She quickly grabbed a few ham sandwiches, a bag of potato chips, and a tub of strawberry yogurt and hustled Bertie to the counter.

She paid cash, and when the cash register drawer opened on its own with a loud ping Bertie jumped backwards, knocking over a pyramid of Pringles.

"Duude," drawled the clerk. "You need to chill. What're you on anyway?"

"He's just from out of town," said Nikki, chasing after Pringles cans as they rolled down the aisle. "He's not left the farm much," she said, waving at Bertie's rough linen shirt and wool trousers.

"Gotcha," said the clerk, tapping his nose. "Amish dude. Had a couple of them in the store last week. Didn't think those dudes drank, but these two young guys bought a whole case of Bud and a six-pack of Pale Ale. I guess when they're off the farm they like to party."

"They have ale here?" asked Bertie with a sudden eager gleam in his eyes.

"No, they do *not*," said Nikki, grabbing her change and shoving Bertie out the door. He was enough of a challenge to manage when he was sober. She couldn't even begin to imagine the trouble a drunk Bertie could get into. She hustled him around the side of the Quik Mart into an alley she sometimes took as a shortcut home. The store had security cameras which normally kept the alley clear of vagrants, but this time she noticed two people huddled between the garbage bins in a way which immediately triggered her suspicions. Drug deal, she thought as she saw a wad of dollar bills change hands. She tried to pull Bertie back out of the alley, but the teenager with the wad of bills looked up.

"Hey!" he shouted, rushing out from between the garbage bins. "You! I know you. You're in my chem class. What're you doing here? Spying on me?"

"Of course not," said Nikki, trying to look calm and in control as she found herself face to face with Bobby Dinsfeld. She tried to look as if spying on him was the last thing she'd ever do, even though only a day ago she'd been hiding in an old, rusty thresher on his family's farm doing exactly that.

"I also know this young lady," said a harsh, creaky voice.

Nikki's eyes widened in astonishment as Fortuna the Fortunate stepped out from behind Bobby.

"Fortuna!" gasped Bertie. "How . . . what . . . how did you get here?"

"The same way you did, dearie," said Fortuna, eyeing him like a con artist sizing up a mark. "My, my. So many old friends suddenly appearing in this odd land. It makes me quite homesick."

Fortuna was fiddling with the multitude of beaded necklaces she wore, rattling them to such an extent that Nikki wondered if she was trying to distract attention from something else. Sure enough, she noticed that Fortuna's other hand was trying to stuff a small paper bag under her shawl. It seemed to be catching on something, and the old fortune-teller went into such contortions that even Bertie noticed.

"I say old girl, are you feeling all right?" he asked, looking alarmed. "Are you ill? Is it catching? I'm hopelessly prone to illness, you know, The slightest cold and I'm on my deathbed."

"I'm fine, dearie," said Fortuna. "Nothing to worry about. Merely the discomforts of old age." She spotted the Quik Mart bag Bertie was carrying. "You couldn't see your way to giving an old woman a morsel of food, could you Your Highness?" she asked. "I've been so very, very hungry." She held out a veined, trembling hand, which immediately closed in a vice-like grip around the bag of potato chips Bertie handed her. The loud crunching sound startled an alley cat which was sniffing around their feet. It yowled and took off like its tail was on fire.

Bobby gave Fortuna an odd look. "Why'd you call this goober Your Highness?" he asked. "He don't look like no King to me. Looks more like one of those Amish morons." He poked Bertie in the chest with a stubby finger. "Where's your horse and buggy, Amish?"

"I say, young man," said Bertie. "There's no call for this physical assault on my person. As to my horse, well, I have several noble steeds. They are all back home in . . ."

Nikki grabbed his arm and tugged at him. "We've got to get going. See you in class, Bobby."

Bobby jumped in front of her. "Hang on, Murrow," he said. "You ain't gonna talk about me and this old lady, are you? About what we were doing? Cause we weren't doing nothing wrong. I don't even know her. I just gave her some money and food, cause she was begging."

"Begging!" gasped Fortuna. "I have never begged for anything in my life. I'll have you know that I am a much respected person in my homeland. My name is known from Castle Cogent to Kingston."

"Castle What?" asked Bobby. "Boy, you're crazier than a bag of snakes, ain't you. Besides, don't tell me you never begged. You just begged for a bag of potato chips. It's still in your hand."

Fortuna put on a regal expression and tucked the bag of chips under her shawl. "I was not begging. I was merely asking a small favor of an old friend."

"Friend?" said Bertie. "That's a bit of a stretch, Fortuna. I am not your friend. I am your King. In fact, I signed a warrant for your arrest. Athena wrote it, but I signed it personally. In the Castle

Cogent throne room."

"What is with all this Castle stuff?" Bobby asked Nikki. "You have some weird friends, Murrow. If I were you I'd stop hanging around with crazy types. They're going to get you in trouble." He pushed his way past Nikki and Bertie and disappeared down the alley.

Nikki folded her arms and stared at Fortuna. "What's in the bag?" she asked.

Fortuna's face tried without success to assume an innocent expression. "What bag, dearie? Do you mean this one?" She ripped open the potato chip bag and hesitantly nibbled at a chip. "What an odd taste. I'm not sure it's to my liking."

"Not that bag, Fortuna," said Nikki. "The one Bobby handed you."

"Bobby?" said Fortuna. "Is that the name of that young man? He didn't hand me any bags. He merely gave me a bit of money, as a favor to an old woman who didn't have quite enough to eat today. I have found a place of employment in this strange land, but it doesn't pay quite as well as I'd hoped."

"He gave you a brown paper bag," said Nikki. "You stuffed it under your shawl."

"Nonsense," said Fortuna. "You are seeing things, my dear. Now, if you'll excuse me, I need to return home and have a rest. Not that my new home is quite as restful as I would like. It is quite overrun with mice I'm afraid. The landlady claims this is due to the presence of something called the Dim Sum Palace next door. I have no idea what Dim Sum is, or why it would attract mice, but I can assure you the establishment is in no way a palace. It is more of a hut in need of a good paint job." She pushed past Nikki, toddled unsteadily out of the alley and disappeared around the corner of the Quik Mart.

Nikki watched her go. She was pretty sure that the bag Bobby had passed Fortuna contained meth. He and Rufius were apparently going to expand their customer base from students at her high school to the city of Madison in general. But Fortuna was an odd choice for the role of drug pusher. Maybe the idea was for her to sell the meth to her psychic clients. Nikki wondered if she should make an anonymous call to the police. Maybe they could raid Fortuna's new place of employment and discover the bag of meth. But that wouldn't solve the problem of Rufius. Fortuna would almost certainly try to implicate him, but Nikki doubted that would work. Fortuna was a cranky old woman working as a psychic. Rufius was a charming young guy with a good job in a high school. He'd have the police on his side in no time. Nikki felt a bit sorry for Fortuna despite her con artist past. She was an old, ailing woman. On her own, without friends or family, in a world completely strange to her. Nikki knew what it was like to be a stranger in another world. She'd spent over a year in the Realm of Reason. But she'd had Fuzz and Athena to guide her, and she was a young and healthy person with no disabilities. Fortuna was having trouble just walking. It was clear that she was rapidly approaching that time in life when she wouldn't be able to care for herself.

Nikki tugged on her hair in frustration. She already had Curio and Bertie depending on her. She was in no position to take care of Fortuna as well.

"Not bad, not bad at all," said Bertie. He was delicately munching on one of the ham sandwiches. "The cheese is perhaps not quite up to Realm standards, but the ham is quite tasty."

"Great," said Nikki. "Look, I need to get back to school. You should be all set now. You've got enough food for today, and you know where to buy more. Tomorrow me and Curio will take you to the pawn shop and show you how to exchange Realm coins for dollars."

"Yes," said Bertie. "About that. It seems I am running through the handful of coins you allowed me at an alarming rate. I lost five of them last night in a card game at that 'Y' establishment. One of the gents there is quite the card sharp. I am no slouch in that department, but the game he invited me to had very different rules than card games in the Realm. I don't suppose you could be so generous as to return my bag of coins to me?"

"No," said Nikki. "Absolutely not. You can't afford to gamble like that, Bertie. Not here. Maybe back in the Realm you could get away with it. There you were the King's nephew, with palaces and the Royal treasury at your disposal. Here you're just an unemployed nobody living at the Y. You need to make your bag of coins last as long as possible. Who knows how long it'll take to get you back through the portal? You could be here for months. Even years. And you're not the only one depending on that bag of coins. Curio needs to live off it as well. I can't afford to support him. I'm only fourteen. I'm still in school and my mom gives me five dollars a week as an allowance. That's not going to keep you in ham sandwiches. So cool it with the gambling. Immediately."

Bertie's pale, expressive face looked both ashamed and petulant at the same time. "But there's nothing to *do* here," he whined, sounding exactly like a bored six-year-old.

Nikki sighed. "I know. I get it. But you're just going to have to deal, Bertie. Our priority has to be Rufius. He's trying to spread a dangerous drug around my school. We have to stop him and get him back through the portal if possible. Now, go back to the Y. Or go for a long walk around the lake. Just stay out of trouble. I have to get back to school before I'm late for my next class."

# Chapter Nine

## Intruder

NIKKI DUMPED HER backpack on her bed and plopped down beside it. It had been a long day. There'd been a test in Calculus II and then a meeting of the debate team after school. She just wanted to close her eyes for a second and take a short nap before dinner. But something was bugging her. It wasn't her worries about Rufius, or Bertie's gambling. No, it was something closer to home. She looked around her bedroom. Everything seemed normal. Her poster of the periodic table was still above the bed. Her bedspread was still crumpled and half falling onto the floor. Her well-worn chemistry and physics textbooks from junior high were still piled on top of her old walnut dresser beneath its cracked mirror. Still, she couldn't shake the feeling that something wasn't quite right. She got up and nudged the empty water glass on her desk an inch to the left. She couldn't swear it had been moved out of place, but the hairs on the back of her neck were standing up. She had the distinct feeling that someone had been in her room.

Her mother almost never came into her bedroom. They both liked space and privacy. Places to think, work, and study. When they got together to talk it was at the dining table or in the living room. Nikki had cleaned her own room and done her own laundry since she was ten. Her mother had checked up on her results a few times, when she was only ten and inclined to skip washing her sheets until they started to smell. But nowadays she trusted Nikki and didn't usually run chore patrol. Nikki spun in a slow circle, half-closing her eyes, watching for anything out of place. There. The bottom drawer of the end table next to her bed was closed. She'd left it open when she'd left for school that morning. She was sure of it. She'd been in a rush, hunting for her calculator. And the end table was the last place she'd looked for it.

She went over and pulled the end table drawer wide open. The same old dried out pens and stubby pencils. The same old notepad full of differential equations. It had a lot of cross-outs and errors, because she'd started trying to teach herself diffy-Q when she was twelve and had not been instantly successful. She opened the other drawers. Just old paperback books and a half-full box of Kleenex. She straightened up and looked around. There was nothing valuable in her room except her microscope, which was still in its place on top of her desk. Her laptop was in her backpack. She'd taken it to school with her.

She walked slowly to her desk and pulled open the top drawer. Yep. One thing was missing. Money. She'd cashed in a handful of Bertie's coins yesterday at the pawn shop. She'd tucked fifty dollars in ones and fives into a baggie and put it in the desk drawer. The baggie was gone. The rest of Bertie's bag of coins was still buried out in the side yard.

Curio was a possible culprit, but he didn't have a key to the apartment. And it just didn't seem like something he'd do. She knew he'd stolen food back in the Realm, but that was pure survival. She couldn't imagine him stealing money from a friend.

She left her bedroom and went into the hall. She opened the front door and knelt down. The door's old brass doorknob had scratches all over it. It was impossible to tell if any of them were recent additions.

She closed the door and went into the living room. The only thing in the room even remotely valuable was their flat-screen TV. It was only a thirty-two incher and it was five years old, still she supposed that a normal thief would have taken it along with her stash of fifty dollars. But it was still there, with a thick coat of dust on its screen.

She sat down on the couch and tugged at her hair, running through possibilities. She supposed that a random burglar was still a possible suspect, but the lack of ransacking seemed to rule it out. A druggie looking for quick cash would have taken a crowbar to the front door and pulled out every drawer in the place. Bobby Dinsfeld was a possibility. His family's farm could be having financial troubles, and he could've found out where she lived by asking someone at school. Despite the stupidity of getting involved with Rufius and meth, Bobby was a smart guy. He wasn't top of their class, but he did okay in AP Chemistry. He was smart enough to teach himself lock-picking.

But something about this didn't seem like Bobby. He was a blunt instrument, and this had finesse written all over it. The way everything in the apartment was untouched except for the missing money. The person who'd taken it knew she'd eventually discover the theft, but perhaps not right away. She might realize the money was missing only after having slept in a burgled apartment for days. It was a sneaky tactic, injecting a hint of fear and uncertainty. It smelled of Rufius.

She thought about the old brass doorknob on the front door. It was original, dating back to the 1920's when the apartment building was built. It was a simple thumb-lock, not a deadbolt. It was probably not too hard to pick. The lock on the lobby door was the same kind. Even Rufius, someone from a land where locks were still of the crude, medieval, skeleton-key type, could probably figure out how to pick it.

Nikki shivered all over. She did *not* want to contemplate the idea of Rufius in the apartment. She jumped up and went into the kitchen to make herself a cup of cocoa. While the water heated she tried to calm down by focusing again on Bobby. Maybe he was sneakier than he seemed. He wasn't exactly an upstanding citizen, but he was better than the alternative. As far as she knew he'd never tried to murder anyone. The same couldn't be said of Rufius. She'd ask around at school tomorrow, try to figure out if Bobby had skipped any classes today. Whoever it was, they'd had a window of opportunity from around eight in the morning until about one in the afternoon. Her mom always got to her lab at the university by nine, but she frequently came home for lunch.

Nikki checked the calendar taped to the fridge. Her mom had a faculty meeting today from 5pm to 7pm. And there was a bowl of chili in the fridge with a post-it on the side which said 'nuke for dinner'. Nikki stuck the bowl in the microwave, put a paper towel over it, and pushed Start. She left the microwave to do its thing, took the front door key from its jade bowl on top of the bookcase in the hall and left the apartment, carefully locking the door behind her. She ran down the stairs to the second-floor apartment and knocked quietly. Curio took a long time to respond, and she was starting to get worried when the door opened a crack and a single blue eye peeped at her.

"Hello, Miss," whispered Curio. "Sorry, I was enjoying that pipe in the ceiling which rains. I don't know how they gets the water so hot. It must take a very big fireplace down in the basement somewheres." He stuck a foot in the doorway, but a furry flash whizzed by and Cation wrapper herself around Nikki's ankles, purring loudly.

Nikki picked her up and motioned to Curio. "Come on. I'll give the two of you a hot dinner for a change. My mom left chili. And I think we have some chocolate cake leftover from a birthday party they had at my mom's office."

Curio shut the door and followed her upstairs. "What should I do if she comes home, Miss?" he asked. "Should I hide in your closet?"

"I guess we can keep that as a backup plan," said Nikki as she unlocked the front door. "But I doubt you'll have to hide. She's at a meeting at the university where she works. She's a chemist."

"What's a chemist, Miss?" asked Curio. "And what's a university?"

"A chemist is someone who studies substances," said Nikki. "She studies atoms and molecules and how they interact with each other. She's an organic chemist, which means she studies carbon-based substances."

"What's atoms and molycues and carbon?" asked Curio.

"Never mind," said Nikki. "Let's have dinner."

Their feast of chili and chocolate cake was quite enjoyable until they realized that chili didn't agree with Cation's digestive system. Curio snatched her up and ran downstairs and left her in the side yard while Nikki got started on the clean-up.

"I still smells it, Miss," said Curio when he returned.

"I know," sighed Nikki, dumping another wad of brown paper towels down the garbage disposal. "Open up all the windows in the living room. I'll wash the kitchen floor with Clorox. At least she kept most of the damage in here." She pulled a mop and bucket out from the closet next to the sink. "How's it going with the litterbox, anyway? Is she making any progress?"

"Oh yes, Miss," said Curio. "Your kitty has been doing her business in that box of sand with no problem. When she's done I digs out her little presents and throws them out the window."

"I hope you've been washing your hands afterwards," said Nikki.

"My hands, Miss?" said Curio, looking down at his tiny hands with their black fingernails.

Nikki rolled her eyes. "Curio, I've *told* you about this. If your hygiene doesn't improve you're not going to make it to your twelfth birthday. You'll get a stomach infection and keel over dead. You probably have whole colonies of bacteria under those fingernails."

Curio brought one hand up so close to his face that he was cross-eyed. "What are backerias? I don't see nothing at all."

"They're small animals," said Nikki, putting the mop and bucket back in the closet. "They're too small to see with the naked eye. Come on, I'll show you. After we *both* wash our hands."

She led Curio into her bedroom and turned on the light under her microscope. She got a Q-tip out of the desk drawer and ran it under one of Curio's fingernails, which were still black despite a thorough cleaning with Dial soap and a hefty dollop of hand sanitizer. She mixed the black gunk with a few drops of distilled water and a drop of methylene blue to Gram-stain it for maximum visibility. She spread the mixture on a glass slide and adjusted the focus on the microscope to a 400x magnification. "Have a look," she said.

Curio eyed her a bit warily, but he bent and looked into the eyepiece. "I don't see nothing, Miss," he said. "Just a bright light."

"Hang on," said Nikki. "Let me try. Sometimes the little buggers are hard to see, or they swim out of view." She swiveled the lens around. "There. Found one. Looks like a protozoa. They're big compared to bacteria, so they're easier to see."

"What's a protozee?" asked Curio, looking at the microscope as if it might come to life and eat him.

"They're single-celled organisms," said Nikki. "Eukaryotes. That just means they have a nucleus in their cell which is enclosed in a membrane. We're also eukaryotes, we just have a lot more than one cell. Come on, have a look quick. Before it swims out of frame."

Curio didn't look happy, but he bent to the eyepiece again. A second later he sprang back, his face as white as a sheet. "It's a monster, Miss! Look at all the tentacles! We should kill it before it gets us!" he looked wildly around the room as if searching for a sword and shield.

"It's not a monster," said Nikki. She sat him down on the bed. "Put your head between your knees before you pass out. Sorry, that was my fault. Protozoa can look a little creepy, but you get used to them."

She went out to the kitchen and brought him back a glass of water. "Here. Drink it slowly and take deep breaths. But not too deep. We don't want you hyperventilating."

"What's that, Miss?" asked Curio between gulps and gasps.

"Never mind," said Nikki. "That's enough new knowledge for one day. Let's go down to the side yard and clean up all the cat doodys you've been throwing out the window. I don't want the smell attracting every tomcat in the neighborhood. That reminds me, Cation might have a long stay here. And she'd not a little kitten anymore. She's close to maturity. I should take her to the animal shelter to get her fixed."

"What's that, Miss?" asked Curio.

Nikki sighed. She was fond of Curio, but she was beginning to feel like a parent with a toddler who asked constant questions. "It's just something for her health. Don't worry about it."

As she locked the front door behind them and headed down the stairs to the lobby she snuck a quick glance at Curio. "Hey," she said, "You didn't happen to go into our apartment this morning, did you?"

Curio came to an astonished halt, one foot dangling above the next step. "No, Miss. Of course not. I don't have no keys to get in. And I wouldn't anyways."

"No, of course you wouldn't," said Nikki. "Forget I asked."

"Okay, Miss," said Curio doubtfully.

It took them quite a while to clean up the side yard. Cation helped by chasing butterflies and winding herself around their ankles. Nikki dug a hole under a rose bush in the far back corner of the yard and they dumped Cation's 'presents' into it and then covered them up with dirt.

While she was digging Nikki mulled over the theft of the fifty dollars from her desk. It was extremely creepy, but it also gave her an idea. Maybe she could also pull off a theft. Her earlier idea about chemically neutralizing the meth created by Bobby had failed, but maybe she could do something simpler. She could just steal it. Steal all of it and then destroy it.

She looked over at Curio, who was methodically walking back and forth across the lawn searching for any remaining presents. She couldn't involve him. It was too dangerous. But it would be a good idea to have help. She didn't know how much of the drug they'd made, and she might need help moving it.

Bertie. It was time for him to earn his keep.

## Chapter Ten

### The Haul

"DO I REALLY need to wear this ridiculous mask?" griped Bertie, pulling at the neck of his ski mask. "I can't breathe in it."

"Yes," said Nikki. "I told you, it's important that no one sees our faces."

"But it's pitch black out here in these blasted woods," said Bertie. "I can't even see my own feet."

"I already explained this," said Nikki. "Our world has things called cameras. Some of them can take a picture of you even in the dark. I didn't see any cameras the last time I was here, but it's better to be safe than sorry. Now be quiet. We're getting close to the shed."

Nikki paused on the edge of the forest, searching the wide expanse of prairie grass in front of her for any sign of movement. She knew that Bobby Dinsfeld was at a Milwaukee Admirals hockey game with his parents. He'd been talking about it all week in chemistry class. Bobby and his parents were the only people who lived in the farm house off in the distance across the fields. Rufius was at a staff meeting at her high school. She'd gone to the school after dinner to check. He'd been sitting in a corner of the teachers' lounge, his feet up on a table, looking bored. The meeting was supposed to last until 8pm. That gave them an hour to grab the meth and dump it in the creek which ran along the Dinsfeld property to the north. The creek emptied into a large marshy area, which should dilute the drug so much that it would be harmless to the local wildlife. At least she hoped it would. Anyway, a duck accidentally ingesting a little bit of meth was much better than a kid from her high school intentionally injecting a lot of it.

She stared at the shed she'd hidden behind only two days ago. It was dark and silent. She could just make out the thresher she'd hidden in. In the dark it looked like some kind of misshapen monster about to attack. She'd thought about just burning the whole shed to the ground, but the chance of the fire spreading through the prairie grass to local houses was just too great.

She pulled a crowbar out of her backpack and stepped out into the prairie grass.

Bertie followed, muttering something inaudible. Its tone was a mixture of whine, fear, and 'Why Me?'. It contrasted strangely with the army camo jacket he was wearing over his Realm clothes. Someone had left it in the used-clothes bin at the Y and Bertie had adopted it. It didn't really go with his refined, delicate build. Nikki thought he looked like he was play-acting. But she supposed that most guys who wore camo looked like they were play-acting.

When she reached the door of the shed Nikki put her ear to it. There was a very faint skittering noise, probably rats, but nothing else. She tried the door handle, but it was locked as expected. She had no skill at lockpicking, so she'd decided on the brute force approach. She hoped that would leave the impression of a random break-in. Madison wasn't a high-crime city, but break-ins did happen sometimes.

She wedged the curved end of the crowbar into the crack between the door and the jamb and pulled. The door creaked a little, but otherwise refused to cooperate. She leaned all her weight back from the crowbar and pulled again. A few splinters dropped into the prairie grass but the door remained stubbornly closed.

"Okay," she whispered to Bertie. "It's time to make yourself useful." She handed him the crowbar.

"This is a ridiculous thing for a King to be engaged in," said Bertie. "As soon as I get back to the Realm I'm going to have the Castle Cogent servants draw me a hot bath and massage me with oil of lavender. There will be no more sleeping in 'Y's' and breaking down doors."

"Just open the door!" hissed Nikki.

Bertie sighed deeply as he inserted the crowbar into the door. After a few pulls the door jamb cracked in two and the door swung inwards. Apparently Bertie felt that his manly duty was done. He stepped aside and let Nikki go in first.

There were squeaks and scurryings as Nikki stepped inside, but no sign of any humans. "Come in and close the door," she whispered to Bertie, tucking the crowbar back into her backpack.

Once the door was shut the darkness was complete. Nikki got a flashlight out of her backpack and switched it on. The shed had two small windows, both covered with blackout paper. There was little chance that anyone outside the shed could see her flashlight. The tiny light flickered over wheelbarrows, rakes, and an old rusty plow. In the middle of the shed a space had been cleared on the dirt floor and a makeshift workbench was set up.

Nikki ignored the plastic buckets and other powder-encrusted tools used to make the meth. She focused her flashlight on a burlap sack about three feet long and two feet wide. It sat on one end of the workbench and was bulging at the seams. Another sack about half its size sat on the floor below it. Both sacks were zip-tied at the top. Nikki pulled a Swiss Army knife out of the pocket of her jeans and ripped a hole in the side of the larger sack. She shone the flashlight into the sack. Ziplock sandwich bags which she recognized from the local Quik Mart were stuffed full of white powder.

Nikki quickly searched the rest of the shed, but found no other sacks. "Okay," she whispered. "You grab the big one and I'll carry the small one."

Bertie sighed but grabbed the large sack by its zip-tied end and tried to lift it. He staggered a few feet with it and then dropped it on the dirt floor. "Nope," he said, folding his arms. "It can't be done. Not by me at least. What you need is a horse for this kind of heavy lifting. Or a donkey. Do I look like a donkey?"

"Well, you're certainly *acting* like a donkey," said Nikki. She tried to lift the small sack. Bertie was unfortunately right. The sacks were stuffed to the gills and very heavy.

"Well, I guess this ends our little adventure," said Bertie. "I'll be at the Y place if you need me. Which hopefully won't be soon. I need a good night's sleep. Last night some drunken fool in the room next to mine was banging on the wall all night and yelling about something called a pickup truck. Apparently he smashed his into something called a stop-light. It seems to have been the stop-light's fault. This Y place you have stuck me in does *not* have the most well-behaved clientele. The Realm has street beggars and pickpockets with more manners."

"You give up too easily, Bertie," said Nikki. She retrieved a wheelbarrow from a dark corner and wheeled it next to the work-bench. "Put the sack in here."

Bertie complied, with much grumbling. "I suppose you want the little one as well," he said.

"Yes," said Nikki. She went to the door and opened it a crack. An owl was hooting in the trees and a few bats were flying in the moon-light, but otherwise everything was still and quiet. She carefully closed the door again. "Does it roll okay?" she asked.

Bertie grasped the handles and wheeled it around the shed. "Not too bad," he said. "But surely you can't expect me to push this thing all the way back to the city. That's miles and miles."

"No," said Nikki. "We're going to dump this stuff in the creek nearby. It's only a hundred yards away."

"Oh," said Bertie. "Well, I guess I can manage that. But then it's off to bed. I get positively cranky when I don't get enough sleep."

"Just be quiet and follow me," said Nikki. She pushed open the door and carefully wiped the door knob clean of any fingerprints. She waved at Bertie and he rolled the wheelbarrow out of the shed.

"Wait here for a second," whispered Nikki. She went back into the shed, grabbed one of the rakes leaning against the back wall, and thoroughly raked the dirt floor of the shed. She trailed the rake after her as she left, then wiped it clean of her fingerprints and dropped it in the grass.

"Odd time to do a bit of gardening," said Bertie. "Personally, I've never been much of a gardening enthusiast. I enjoy picking a few roses in the spring, but grubbing about in the dirt with the worms has never appealed to me."

"I'm erasing any trace of who was here," said Nikki. "Especially my footprints. It's easy to see they're a child's or a woman's. I want Rufius and Bobby to think this was a random break-in. I don't want them tracing it back to me. Now, come on. The creek is this way."

It was relatively easy going while they were in the prairie grass, but when they hit the bumpy undergrowth of the forest Bertie started to complain bitterly.

"I can't," he wheezed. "I just can't push it one inch farther." He dropped the handles of the wheelbarrow and collapsed on a fallen log.

Nikki resisted the urge to kick him. She stopped and listened. The trickling of water was just barely audible. "We're near the creek," she said. "Wait here." She headed for a thick hedge of alder trees which stood out from the rest of the pine woods like a black wall. Alders tended to cluster on the banks of streams and rivers, and these were no exception. She stepped in the creek before she saw it. She pulled her foot out of the marshy ground with difficulty and walked along the edge of the thick band of shrub-like alders, trying to find a way to deeper water. But it was no use, she kept sinking into the muddy ground. She walked the few yards back to Bertie.

"We're going to have to do this bag by bag," she said, pulling out her knife and slitting the large burlap sack open. "Grab an armful of these and follow me."

She grabbed four of the sandwich bags and returned to the edge of the marshy creek. She pushed her way through the hedge of alders, found the firmest ground she could, and dropped the bags. She slit each one open and poured its contents into the creek.

"Drop them here," she said as Bertie appeared. "Then go get more. You carry, I'll dump."

She soon had a stack of deflated sandwich bags in the grass next to her, as well as a splitting headache. The breeze was lifting some of the powder into the air each time she split open a bag. She pulled her ski mask up over her nose and wished she'd thought to bring a medical-grade N95 mask.

"This is the last of them," said Bertie, dropping eight sandwich bags next to her.

Nikki nodded and held her breath as she quickly split and dumped the last bags. She gathered up the empty sandwich bags and stuffed them in her backpack. She swayed as she got to her feet, but managed to make it back to the fallen log Bertie had sat on. She sat down on the log, holding her head. "Take the wheelbarrow back to the shed. It was propped against the back wall. I'll . . ." Her head spun and she twisted and vomited over the side of the log.

"Oh my goodness," gasped Bertie. "Are you ill? Should I run for a healer? Do you even *have* healers in this world?"

"Of course we have healers in this world," said Nikki, wiping her mouth. "They're called doctors. And I don't need one. I just breathed in a little of the drug. I'll be fine in a minute. Go return the wheelbarrow."

Bertie stared at her uncertainly for a few moments, but when Nikki showed no sign of keeling over dead he shrugged and trundled away with the wheelbarrow.

Nikki wasn't feeling quite as well as she'd pretended to in front of Bertie. As soon as he was out of earshot she vomited again. It was hard to tell in the dark, but her eyesight seemed fuzzy and out of focus. Maybe she did need to see a doctor. She pulled off her soiled mask and forced herself to stand, staggering a few feet before walking into a tree. She fell to the ground, her head spinning. She tried to pull herself to her knees, but it was too much. She crashed back to the ground, unconscious among the muddy leaves.

"WHAT . . .?" Nikki mumbled. "Where . . .?"

"Shhhh," whispered Bertie. "Just stay still. We're almost back to the city."

Nikki struggled to open her eyes. For some reason the left one was determined to stay shut. Above her Bertie's face swam in and out of focus. "Why am I bouncing up and down?" she asked.

"Sorry," said Bertie. "I'm trying not to jostle you, but the ground in this cornfield is extremely uneven."

"Oh," said Nikki. Bertie was carrying her. She managed to get both eyes open and looked around. Her vision was beginning to clear. That was a good sign. Her head hurt, but at least the world wasn't spinning anymore. "Put me down," she said. "I think I can walk now."

Bertie set her carefully on her feet, keeping one arm around her back.

Nikki squirmed out of his grasp and toddled forward a few feet. "Not too bad," she said. "I don't feel like running a marathon, but I think I can make it home."

Bertie nodded and they walked in silence through the cornfield.

Nikki stopped when they came to a deserted two-lane country road. "This is Highway 20, I think. And Madison's over that way, obviously, from all the lights. It's a lot closer than I thought it would be. You must have been walking for quite a while."

"About an hour, I think," said Bertie. "We'd be back in the city already, but I tried to keep to the fields and avoid the roads, so it was slow going. I was afraid Rufius might have come to his senses and was out on the roads searching for us."

"Come to his senses?" said Nikki.

"Yes," said Bertie. "He sprang up out of the prairie grass like a tiger and jumped on me when I reached the shed. He must have arrived while we were at the creek. We exchanged fisticuffs, and he was getting the better of me, but I happened to put my hand on that rake you left in the grass. I hit him on the head with it and he went down like a toppled statue."

"Did he know it was you?" asked Nikki.

Bertie shook his head. "No, I don't think so. I still had that extremely uncomfortable mask on, and I was careful not to speak."

Nikki breathed a sigh of relief. "Well, that's something to be grateful for."

They walked in silence along the deserted road. Farm houses started to appear, dark and set back from the road. Then rows of tract housing started to replace the corn fields. A TV blared from someone's window.

"He was alive when you left him, wasn't he?" Nikki asked suddenly.

"Yes," said Bertie. "I checked. He was breathing. Not that his passing would sadden me in the slightest, but I don't fancy living the rest of my life as a murderer."

"It would have been a clear case of self-defense," said Nikki.

"I suppose," said Bertie. "Still, I'd rather not have something like that on my conscience."

"You fought against the Knights of the Iron Fist when they tried to take over Cogent Town," said Nikki.

"Yes, I did," said Bertie. "But they were armed thugs who were ravaging and destroying like rabid dogs. I saw them going after children. Children! We had no choice but to put them down."

"Rufius was their leader," said Nikki.

"I know," said Bertie. "And believe me, I thought about that when I saw him lying on the ground back there at that shed. I could easily have killed him. It would have solved many problems, both here and in the Realm."

"But it would have been wrong," said Nikki.

"Yes," sighed Bertie.

"Take off that jacket," said Nikki, looking at Bertie as they passed under a streetlight.

"What?" asked Bertie in surprise.

"Your camo jacket," said Nikki. "It's too distinctive. Rufius probably got a look at it in the moonlight, when you were fighting."

"Oh," said Bertie, pulling off his jacket. "Its lining appears to be a solid color. Dark green, I think." He turned the jacket inside-out and put it back on. "How is this?"

"That'll work," said Nikki. "What did you do with your mask?"

"It's right here," said Bertie, pulling it out of a pocket.

Nikki took it and stuffed it in her backpack. Her own mask was back by the fallen log where she'd passed out. Rufius or Bobby might find it, but there was nothing about it which could be traced back to her.

They reached the city center twenty minutes later. It was well past rush hour and only a few cars were going by on State Street. Groups of students from the nearby University of Wisconsin were wandering around aimlessly, laughing and smelling of weed.

Nikki stopped at an intersection. "The Y is that way," she said, pointing down State Street toward the state capital building. "I don't need to tell you to be even more careful now. Rufius is going to be furious about the stolen meth."

"He has no proof that I had anything to do with that," said Bertie.

"I doubt he'll care," said Nikki. "You'll make a really convenient target for his rage. Me, I have lots of people who know me here. My mom, her work colleagues, the students at my school, my teachers. I'm sure Rufius realizes that attacking me could get him into serious trouble. But you, you're just a guy nobody knows, staying at the Y. If you were to disappear it's likely no one would notice."

"How very comforting," said Bertie. "I advise you not to become a healer. Your patients would likely die just to get away from you."

"I'm just trying to get you to be careful," said Nikki. "We don't know each other all that well, but I do care what happens to you."

Bertie just sniffed and turned away, walking as if there were lead weights attached to his feet. He only made it half a block before he suddenly came running back.

"I can't face that blasted Y," he said. "Rufius is staying there. He'll break into my room and murder me in my sleep. Please let me stay with you."

"I don't know. . ." said Nikki.

"*Please*," said Bertie.

Nikki sighed, already feeling like she was going to regret this. "You'd have to be very, *very* quiet."

"Yes, of course," said Bertie, nodding eagerly.

"And no whining or complaining," said Nikki.

Bertie nodded.

"And Curio would be in charge," said Nikki.

"What!?" said Bertie. "Curio is a child. I am King of the Realm."

"You're not King here," said Nikki. "And Curio's better than you at fitting in."

## Chapter Eleven

### One Big Happy Family

"STOP," SAID NIKKI. They had reached her apartment building and Bertie was heading straight for the front entrance. "Follow me. We have to go through a hole under the hedge."

"Not this again," whined Bertie. "The last time I did this the scratches on my back itched for a week. Can't we just go in the front door?"

"No," said Nikki. "My mom's probably home by now. We can't risk running into her on the stairs."

"Why?" asked Bertie. "Is she a horrible person?"

"Of course not," said Nikki. "But how the heck am I going to explain to her why I'm letting a strange man into the building? Now shut up and follow me."

She squirmed quickly under the hedge. Bertie followed more slowly, cursing under his breath.

Nikki looked up at the second-floor windows. She thought she could just make out a tiny flicker from Curio's flashlight. She picked up a pebble from the gravel border at the edge of the lawn and threw it at the window where the light was flickering.

The window creaked open and a small blond head poked out. "Hello, Miss," said Curio. "Yer out late tonight."

"Throw down the rope," whispered Nikki.

Curio nodded and a moment later a coil of rope flew out the window and unfurled against the ivy-covered wall.

Nikki was getting used to the climb and quickly swarmed up the rope, using her legs as much as her arms. When she reached the window a hand much too big to be Curio's suddenly reached out and grabbed her arm. She gasped and nearly let go of the rope in surprise. The hand grabbed the back of her jacket and hauled her into the room.

"Don't be scared, Miss," said Curio. "It's just Mr. Krill."

"Oh, my gosh!" gasped Nikki, her heart beating frantically. "Curio, you should have warned me. I thought it was Rufius."

"Sorry, Miss," said Curio. "Yer getting so quick at climbing the rope that I didn't have time. Miss Kira is here as well."

A black girl a few years older than Nikki stepped forward, her long braids wrapped in blue satin ribbons which gleamed in the moonlight. "Hello, Nikki. It's good to see you again."

"Kira!" gasped Nikki, rushing forward to give the girl a hug. Kira still smelled faintly of the sea and the ship which she and Krill called home. Nikki looked around the room, wondering if there were any more surprise visitors from the Realm.

"Sorry," said Kira. "It's just me and Krill."

"Oh," said Nikki, trying to keep the disappointment out of her voice.

Kira laughed and patted Nikki's arm. "I suppose you were hoping to see Fuzz and Athena."

"Well, yes," said Nikki. "It's great to see you, don't get me wrong. But ever since Curio came through the portal I've been hoping Fuzz and Athena would come through and take charge of things. Rufius is here, as you probably know. And he's causing all kinds of trouble."

"I should just hunt him down and punch him in the face," said Krill, helping Bertie through the window.

"As usual my brother is leading with his fists rather than his brain," said Kira.

Krill grinned. "Sometimes the situation calls for fists," he said, slapping Bertie on the back. "What about it, your Highness? How about you and me go find Rufius and beat some sense into him?"

"Umm," said Bertie. "Well. . ."

"No," said Nikki. "You'll just get arrested by our police. They're like your Rounders, back in the Realm. The two of you in jail isn't going to fix things. Come on, let's all sit down and talk." She shut both the window and the door of Curio's bedroom to block any sound getting out. She and Kira sat on Curio's sleeping bag, Curio sat on the old parka Nikki had given him, and Krill stretched out on the wooden floor. Bertie leaned against the windowsill, looking like he didn't want any part in the conversation.

"So," said Nikki. "Why did the two of you come through the portal, and not Rounders or castle guards?"

"Well," said Kira, "The Rounders and guards have been very busy lately. You see, there are still many Knights of the Iron Fist hiding out in the forests south of Cogent Town. Athena gave the order to round them up for trial."

"Athena gave the order?" said Nikki. "Is she the Queen now?"

"No," said Kira. "She's acting as Regent. As a stand-in for the King while he's gone." She gave Bertie a very hard stare.

Bertie suddenly became extremely interested in looking out the window.

"Things have not been easy in the Realm," said Kira. "The attempted coup led by Rufius caused a lot of havoc and destruction, especially in Cogent Town, Kingston, and ImpHaven. Athena has been running things from Castle Cogent, with Fuzz managing networks of spies and informants to gather information. It's been very difficult for them. There are many people in the Realm who don't want to take orders from imps. These people have grown bolder and more aggressive ever since Rufius stirred up so much anti-imp hatred.

Groups of them gather every day in front of the gates of Castle Cogent, demanding to be let in to see the King." She stared at Bertie again.

"The people of the Realm don't know that Bertie went through the portal?" asked Nikki.

Kira shook her head. "No. Most of them don't even know about the existence of the portal. There've been rumors about it for years, but as you know it tends to be hard to see. Most of the time the alley where it's located looks just like a regular alley. The people living nearby use it to store hay for their donkeys. Anyway, Athena asked me and Krill if we'd be willing to stay in Cogent Town for a while and keep watch in the alley. To see if the portal re-opened. Griff and most of her crew have returned to Kingston, to help the Prince of Physics restore order there. We wanted to go too, but decided that we'd be more use in Cogent Town."

"*You* decided, you mean," said Krill with a bit of grumble in his voice.

Kira sighed. "Yes, all right. *I* decided. Krill wanted to go back to Kingston because there's been a lot of hand-to-hand fighting in the streets there. Apparently he thinks getting a Knight's sword stuck in his gut would be lots of fun."

"They can't stick you if they can't catch you," said Krill. "Me and a few of my mates from our ship were gonna go fishing. We were gonna climb onto the rooftops of Kingston and drop fishing nets on them. Then while they were flopping around like flounders we'd bash 'em on the head. It would've worked."

"Maybe," said Kira. "But you're forgetting about the archers. The Knights of the Iron Fist have expert archers in their ranks. They would have picked you off the rooftops like falcons swooping down on sparrows."

Krill just snorted.

"So," Kira continued, "me and Krill agreed to be on portal patrol.

We basically moved into its alley in Cogent Town. We slept there and ate there and got really bored there. Staring at a blank wall all day is not fun."

"Yeah, Daisy hated it," said Curio. "Donkeys don't mind standing around all day doing nothing, but try to get them to stare at a wall and they kick up a fuss. Daisy never actually kicked me, but she tried a few times. Can't say as I blame her. It *was* really boring work. I just got lucky. I'd been on portal watch for only three days when it appeared. I'm guessing that you two did exactly what I did. You just jumped in when it opened, cause you were afraid it'd close if you ran up to the castle to tell someone."

"Yes," said Kira. "We noticed a funny little glowing spot on the wall, and before we were sure what it was it grew into a darkish hole, about three feet wide. I told Krill to run up to the castle as fast as he could, to inform Athena. I was going to jump in."

"And I told her that *I* should do the jumping," said Krill. "And that *she* should do the informing."

"While we were arguing about it the hole started to get smaller," said Kira. "We were afraid it was going to disappear entirely, so we both jumped in."

"They appeared in the same place I did," said Curio. "In that closet in your place of learning, Miss. I was hanging around there today, dodging that old guy who cleans the floors, not really sure what to do with meself. I thought I'd just watch inside the closet for a while, maybe get lucky, and sure enough, they just popped through that old metal thing with the coal dust all over it. I brought them back here a few hours ago."

Everyone looked expectantly at Nikki.

"Yes, well," said Nikki, feeling her face turn red from everyone staring. "You did the right thing. I guess everyone will just have to stay here for now. I don't really have any other ideas. My idea of putting Bertie in the Y didn't work out very well. Rufius is staying there, for one thing."

Krill jumped up. "Well then what are we waiting for? Let's go get him." He headed for the window. "Come on your Highness. Between the two of us we should be able to handle one ruffian. You three little ones stay here."

"Wait!" said Nikki and Kira at the same time.

"What?" said Krill.

"Are you willing to commit cold-blooded murder?" Nikki asked quietly. "Because that is really your only option. You can't turn Rufius over to our police. As far as they know he hasn't committed any crime. And you can't send him back through the portal to face justice in the Realm, because we have no way of opening the portal from this side."

"We could lock him up somewhere, I guess," said Krill, looking at Bertie.

Bertie just shrugged.

"Where?" said Nikki. "And even if that were possible, you realize you might have to watch him and feed him for weeks, months, maybe even years."

"Years?" said Krill, plopping back down on the floor looking defeated.

Nikki nodded. "Yes, years. We have no way to open the portal. We've tried." She frowned, thinking. "It's odd, you know. Athena and Fuzz seemed to have no trouble opening it a year ago, when they took me to the Realm."

"Athena says that the portal seems to be less reliable now," said Kira. "She told me that she and Fuzz used to use it in years past, to journey to other realms, not just yours. They used it to seek out new knowledge, as our Realm was turning its back on knowledge and favoring superstition. Years ago they were able to rely on the portal, but now it seems to be fading away."

"Well, I hope it will open one last time," said Nikki. "So you can all go back home. And so we can shove Rufius back through it. We have *got* to get him out of my world. He's causing a huge amount of trouble. In the meantime, let's talk about living arrangements. I can get you all some sleeping bags, and Curio and Bertie are somewhat familiar with our local currency and how to buy food. I have to go to school every day, so I'll put Curio in charge of getting you used to things here. The main thing to remember is that you have to be extremely quiet when you're in this apartment. No one's supposed to be in here. Fortunately the only person who might notice you is my mom, because we live one floor above you. The elderly lady downstairs is very hard of hearing. It's unlikely she'd notice anything. And it's really only when my mom is on the stairs that you have to worry. Once she's in our apartment she can't really hear much going on down on the second floor. I'll see if maybe I can rig up some kind of warning system, for when she comes into the building. Something rigged to the front door, which maybe turns on a light in here."

She paused to study Kira and Krill. Krill was wearing a long, patched suede vest over a linen shirt that had seen too many washings. His long legs were encased in leather pants which protected him from the harsh winds of the sea and the rough, scratchy ropes of his ship's rigging. Kira was wearing a long woolen tunic embroidered with lilacs and roses, and heavy linen pants.

"Curio and Bertie stuck out too much when they first arrived here," said Nikki. "As you can see I had to get them some of our clothes so people wouldn't notice them. But you guys don't look that out of place, especially here in this neighborhood where we're close to the university. The students tend to wear all kinds of crazy outfits, and you two actually look kind of cool. But I'll see what I can pick up at Goodwill, just so you have a change of outfits. You'll at least need something to change into when you're washing your clothes. By the way, you can't use the washing machines down in the basement to clean your clothes. The machines make a lot of racket. So much that even old Mrs. Evanston down on the first floor can hear it. And they drive her dog Rocky crazy. He starts barking as soon as you turn them on."

"What's a washing machine?" asked Kira.

"I think I knows," said Curio, looking pale. "Is it more of them iron monsters that prowl yer streets?"

Nikki sighed. "I thought you were getting used to them," she said. "And I told you, they're not monsters, they're cars. We use them the same way people in the Realm use wagons. It's just that cars are faster and louder. And no, washing machines aren't cars. They're just kind of like big tubs filled with water. They spin the water around really fast to get the clothes clean."

"What makes them spin?" asked Kira. "Do you have a water-wheel in your house? I didn't see a stream or river nearby."

"We use a different type of power," said Nikki. "Electricity, not water. But that's a discussion for another time. I can't teach you all about my world in a few minutes, and it's getting late. I need to get upstairs before my mom starts to worry. I'm already out later than I'm supposed to be. But there's one more thing we need to talk about, and that's money. I'm only fourteen, and kids my age don't usually work. We go to school. So I don't have much money to share with you. Curio and Bertie have been living off the bag of Realm coins which Bertie brought with him. But that isn't going to last forever, especially if you guys need to stay here for months or years until the portal opens again. So here's what I'm thinking: Krill can get a job. He's the best candidate. Curio's way too young. Bertie is still struggling to fit in here. Kira, you're a little too young for a full-time job, so people will ask if you have a work permit. That could get really complicated. I'm not even sure how to apply for one. But Krill looks old enough to get full-time work without one. How old are you anyway?"

"Seventeen," said Krill.

"Oh," said Nikki. "You look older. At least eighteen. Probably because of your height. Well, it's not great that you're underage, but there are some jobs that kind of bend the rules about these things. Farm work. Construction. Those kind of physical labor jobs tend to have a lot of turnover and a lot of job openings. And they sometimes aren't fussy about paperwork. They're less likely to ask you for ID than an office job would be. It would be pretty hard work, but hopefully you won't have to do it for too long. What do you think?"

Krill shrugged. "It sounds fine to me. It's better than being stuck in this room with nothing to do. And I'm used to hard work. Hauling in nets full of codfish is no joke."

"Great," said Nikki. "I'll ask around at school. I know a few kids who do part-time farm work." She got up off the floor. "Okay. Curio, I'm depending on you to run things down here. Remember to keep everyone quiet." She looked pointedly at Bertie.

Curio jumped up. "No problems, Miss. We'll all be quiet as mice."

"Speaking of mice," said Nikki, "where's Cation?"

"She's out hunting, Miss," said Curio. "I let her down in her basket around noontime."

"Oh, okay," said Nikki. "How are you doing on cat food? Do you need more?"

"Don't worry about that, Miss," said Curio, standing tall and looking proud of himself. "I boughts a whole bunch of it. A whole box of them little metal cans. I even got coins back." He dug into the pocket of his jeans and pulled out three quarters and a nickel. "I still don't sees how that store makes any money if they gives customers valuable coins in trade for those pieces paper."

Nikki picked one of the quarters out of his palm. "Curio, this is called a quarter. That's because it's worth only a quarter of a dollar bill." She pulled a few coins and a small wad of bills out of her own pocket and spread the money out on the floor. "Look, everyone. This is our currency. Pay attention, cause you'll all need to know this. I know you only have metal coins in the Realm, and aren't used to paper money, but here in my world the paper is much more valuable than the coins. I don't want you giving someone a twenty for a pack of gum and forgetting to get change. That kind of mistake could run through Bertie's bag of gold really quick."

"What's gum, Miss?" asked Curio.

"Never mind," said Nikki. "Pay attention. This is a one-dollar bill. See? There's a number one in the corner. This piece of paper is worth four times what the quarter is worth. And this is a ten-dollar bill. It's worth ten times the one-dollar bill and forty times what the quarter is worth. When you're paying for food and stuff always check the number on the bill before handing it over."

Kira and Krill looked like they didn't quite believe her about the value of the pieces of paper on the floor, but they each picked up a bill and dutifully examined it.

Curio pulled out a few crumpled bills from his pocket, smoothed them out, and with great concentration put all the bills on the floor in order of value and studied them like he was trying to pass a test. "I don't see none of them twenties you was mentioning, Miss," he said. "Is it cause they're really rare?"

"No," said Nikki. "They're pretty common. Just be careful when you're spending them. For example, you should be able to buy dinner at a grocery store for the four of you for about twenty dollars. Just remember to check the price of something before you buy it."

"Oh!" said Curio. "I knows all about prices, Miss. Them little tags with the numbers on them are quite handy. But yer storekeepers here are very grumpy about haggling. In the Realm every shopkeeper learns in their cradle how to haggle. But when I asked the shopkeeper here to knock a bit off the cost of Cation's food he called me a dumb kid and told me to get out of his store. Fortunately there was another shopkeeper there. I think she was the grumpy man's wife, which makes me kind of sorry for her. Anyways, I did the poor little pedestal baby thing and she gave me a very nice price."

Krill laughed. "That settles it. I'll go find work to bring in money and Curio will do all the shopping."

# Chapter Twelve

## Rhetoric

IT WAS A Saturday, but Nikki was out the door and on her way to school by 8am. She still had a headache from breathing in meth, but staying in bed wasn't an option. The debate team had a tournament coming up and the team was scheduled to practice every weekend until then. There were a few cars clustered around the school's auditorium when she arrived. She spotted Tina's red Toyota near the side door, half-hidden behind some discarded scenery from the school's failed attempt to stage The Sound of Music. Her school didn't have a good music department and the auditorium was used mostly for pep rallies for the football team.

"Finally," snapped Tina, when Nikki pushed through the curtain at the back of the stage. "You're late. You were supposed to be here at 8:30."

Nikki glanced at the clock on the back wall of the auditorium. "Chill, Tina. I'm only five minutes late. And besides, hardly anyone's here yet."

"That's because they're all slackers," said Tina. "I expect more from you. And by the way, why aren't you wearing your Westlake Debate Team t-shirt? It shows team spirit."

"Tina, you're not my mother, my boss, or one of my teachers," said Nikki. "So stop bossing me around. And you're the only one who ever wears the team t-shirt to practice debates."

"I'm team captain," said Tina, pulling a compact out of her purse and checking her makeup. "I have to set a good example. And I'll boss you around as much as I want." She put on an extra coat of lipstick and shot a flirty glance at the front row of seats in the dark auditorium.

Nikki squinted at the seats, but the stage lights were in her eyes. She could just make out a dark figure in the center of the front row. "Who is that?" she asked.

"The new guidance counselor," said Tina, putting on more mascara. "He is *such* a cutie. He reminds me of Zac Efron, only taller."

"You said he was a poser," said Nikki, trying to ignore the panicked feeling racing from her brain down to her stomach.

"When did I say that?" asked Tina.

"In chem class," said Nikki.

"Well, I think it's pretty creepy that you go around memorizing everything I say," said Tina. "You need to get some hobbies. Keep busy."

"Tina," said Nikki, "I'm in an empty school auditorium at 8:30 in the morning on a Saturday. I'm busy enough."

Tina just shrugged and gave at little wave toward the front row.

"What's he doing here anyway?" asked Nikki.

"He said he's just getting familiar with all of the school's clubs and extracurriculars. I think it shows a lot of initiative. Most of the teachers don't know we even *have* clubs and extracurriculars."

"He's not a teacher," said Nikki.

Tina shrugged. "Same difference."

There were chairs on the stage, left over from a recital by the school's orchestra. Tina dragged six of them to the front of the stage and arranged them in a semi-circle facing the audience.

"Now," said Tina, "I'm first speaker on our team, you're second. I haven't decided who's third yet. Mr. Tomlinson wants Tim or Anna, but I want Melanie. She's not the sharpest, but she has great stage presence. When she gets on a roll she can really impress the judges, especially the stupid ones. And let's face it, this is a minor tournament. The judges aren't going to be crack attorneys who argue before the Supreme Court. They're going to be librarians and real estate agents judging high school debate contests in their spare time. The team from Southside is pretty good, but they're mostly freshmen, so they're inexperienced. I heard a rumor that their debate teacher was involved in some scandal and all the seniors quit the team. Nasty business. Apparently their teacher hit on some of the girls on the team."

"Ick," said Nikki.

"Yes," said Tina. "But very lucky for us. The seniors on their team were really good, and probably would have wiped the floor with us. But now we have a chance to move on to the district championship if we win this tournament. The topic is *Can Our Senses Be Trusted*, and that plays to Melanie's strengths. It isn't super difficult, intellectually speaking, so she can coast on her acting skills and her voice projection. Which is something you need to work on, Murrow. No one's better than you at pointing out the logical fallacies in an opponent's arguments, but you need to work on your stage presence. Brutally sharp logic is no use if no one can hear your squeaky little voice."

Nikki ignored this. It was an insult that Tina was fond of, and there was some truth to it, though she wasn't going to tell Tina that. Tina's jabs were not high on her priority list just then. She was too busy trying to ignore Rufius and keep an eye on him at the same time. He had left his seat and was walking along the front of the stage toward the stairs. Nikki froze. If he came up on stage should she run? She looked desperately at the sliver of backstage visible between the gap in the curtains. A few members of the debate team were hanging around back there, eating breakfast and avoiding Tina.

Nikki was edging toward backstage, about to make an excuse to Tina about being hungry, when Mr. Tomlinson suddenly pushed through the curtains.

"All right team," he yelled, clapping his hands. "You've had enough Starbucks and Doritos. Honestly, do your parents know how you eat? It's amazing your brains can function at all with all that junk food."

The rest of the team straggled on stage and grumpily pulled up chairs. Mr. Tomlinson handed out sheets of paper and Rufius sat back down in the front row.

"As you can see," said Mr. Tomlinson, "the topic of our upcoming tournament will be *Can Our Senses Be Trusted.* This one's kind of a double-edge sword. It can be approached in a very detailed, scientific way, leaning on the latest advances in neuroscience such as functional magnetic resonance imaging. Focusing on how our sensory perceptions are processed in the brain." He nodded at Nikki.

"Or, it can be approached in a performative, emotion-centric way," he said, nodding at Melanie. "This is the approach I'd like to emphasize. I've chatted up all the judges, and the head judge is the owner of a local car dealership. He loves to write op-eds in the local papers about how young people should avoid studying science because it turns them into robots. I'm exaggerating a bit, but let's just say that he is not an intellectual giant. He'll respond favorably to a comforting, emotional approach that reassures him that he can trust his own eyes and ears."

"Okay," said Nikki. "But we're supposed to be learning how to debate. How to pick apart the flaws in an argument. I don't see how being 'emotionally comforting' is going to accomplish that."

A few members of the debate team nodded in agreement, but Tina let out a huge sigh and threw her hands in the air.

"We want to *win*, Murrow," she said. "And Mr. Tomlinson's approach will help us do that. Geez, you just don't learn, do you? There's more to debate than just logic. Remember last year? When you cost us the state championship because you got a humungous case of stage fright? Stop trying to prove how smart you are and work on your stagecraft."

Nikki felt her face turning red. She wanted to argue back, but she knew Tina had a point. She wasn't good in front of an audience. It was the reason she was on the debate team in the first place. Her mother had encouraged her to join in order to get better at public speaking. It hadn't helped all that much, and she was dreading facing a really big audience again, like the one at the state championships.

Tina stared at her in exasperation, expecting Nikki to say something. When she didn't Tina threw up her hands again.

"I think we should change the line up," said Tina. "Tim should take Nikki's spot as second speaker."

"It's a bit late to make such a big change," said Mr. Tomlinson. "Tim, would you be okay with this?"

"Sure," said Tim, "if Nikki wouldn't mind helping me with research."

"It's settled then," declared Tina. "Nikki can help with the research for the whole team and the line up will be me, Tim, and Melanie."

Nikki sat staring at the floor. Though she knew Tina was right it was still a shock to be kicked off the line up. Especially in front of everybody. When she looked up half the team avoided her glance in embarrassment and the rest looked at her with pity. Her eyes welled up and she quickly ducked her head and pretended to study the sheet of paper Mr. Tomlinson had handed out.

Mr. Tomlinson coughed uncomfortably. "All right, well. If we're all in agreement then let's press on. Let's get started with a practice debate. Tina, you, Tim, and Melanie will argue the affirmative. Nikki, you, Allan, and Jamal will argue the negative. You have fifteen minutes to talk over your approach."

Nikki quickly blew her nose, wiped her eyes, and dragged her chair over to Allan and Jamal.

Allan moved his skateboard out of her way and Jamal gave her a quick thumbs up. She and Jamal were both in AP Chemistry and sometimes collaborated on projects.

"Okay," she said. "I'll let you guys deal with the 'emotional comfort' aspect of the topic. I'll focus on the science. Despite what Mr. Tomlinson said about the head judge, I don't think we should go for completely fluff-headed stuff. Optical illusions are a good entry into the topic. They're science-based, but not too hard to understand."

Jamal pulled out a pen and notebook. "Give me an example," he said.

Nikki thought for a second. "Well, there's the way a stick appears to bend when it's half-in and half-out of water. It's due to the refraction of light. The index of refraction is different for different substances. It measures the bend of a ray of light as it passes from air to water, for example. The index of refraction is calculated using Snell's Law. For air I think it's about 1.0003, and for water it's about 1.333. Denser substances like water have a higher index of refraction, which causes the light to bend more. That'd be an example of a type of optical illusion called a physical illusion. It's caused by the external environment, in this case the way light rays bend when passing through different substances. Anyway, it would be an example of how we can't always trust our senses. The sense in this case being eyesight, of course."

Both Jamal and Allan were shaking their heads vigorously.

"Give us a break, Murrow," said Allan. "We can't memorize all that in fifteen minutes."

"I could, maybe," said Jamal. "But it's not what Mr. Tomlinson is looking for. Haven't you got anything less science-y?"

"How about the classic duck-versus-rabbit illusion?" said Nikki. "Nearly everyone's seen that one, even owners of car dealerships. It's a type of optical illusion called perceptual organization. Our brain tries to organize incoming data from our senses, in this case our eyes, and sometimes fails. It can't decide whether we're seeing a picture of a duck or a picture of a rabbit."

Jamal nodded. "That's more like it." He drew a quick sketch of a duck in his notebook. "We should have an example of a failure of another sense, like hearing or touch."

Nikki nodded. "There was this exhibit at the science museum in Milwaukee. You put your hand on a rubber pad which vibrates at different speeds. If you turn the speed up really high it's too fast for the nerves in your hand to feel it. It's moving really fast but your hand thinks it's completely stationary. It's really weird."

Jamal drew a sketch of a hand in his notebook. "So, we've got two concrete, easy to understand examples of how we can't always trust our sense of sight or our sense of touch. I'll take the vibration example, Allan can have the duck versus rabbit, and I guess you can cover the index of refraction example if you want, Nikki."

Nikki nodded and sat for a few minutes with her eyes closed, trying to organize her argument. She always found this easier to do if she could write her ideas down, but there wasn't time. She was pretty good at thinking on her feet, but the performance aspect of a debate was always a stumbling block for her. Even practice debates made her nervous. She just didn't like people watching her. She opened her eyes and looked over at Melanie, who was doing vocal exercises at top volume and striding around the stage like she owned it. Nikki had a sudden urge to throw a pencil at her head. But she resisted. That was a Tina move, and the last thing she wanted was to become a Tina clone.

Mr. Tomlinson walked to the center of the stage. "All right everyone. Take your places and let's begin."

Tina hopped up. She'd been sitting on the edge of the stage, dangling her legs and talking to Rufius, who was still seated in the front row. "Mr Tomlinson," she said, "why don't we ask Mr. Radnor to be the judge. It would good for us to practice in front of someone new."

Nikki looked around, wondering who the heck Mr. Radnor was. Then she realized that Tina was talking about Rufius. To her horror Rufius left his seat and walked up the steps onto the stage.

He had a new suit on. This one was electric blue, in the same sixties-rock-star style as the purple one he'd had on when he came into her chemistry class. He wore it well, but Nikki noticed that the elbows of the jacket were frayed and so were the pant cuffs. In place of the sandals he used to wear in the Realm of Reason he was now sporting a pair of battered boots just high-heeled enough to look cool but just low enough to avoid looking feminine. She guessed that he was shopping at Goodwill and wondered what his money situation was. She was pretty sure that she and Bertie had destroyed all of the meth he'd stored on the Dinsfeld farm before he'd had chance to sell any. And she doubted that high school guidance counselors made very much money. Especially one with no experience.

Nikki took her place in the semi-circle of chairs facing the auditorium. Mr. Tomlinson dragged two chairs to center-stage and he and Rufius sat down facing the students. Rufius gave Tina a knowing grin and Tina's pale cheeks turned as red as her hair. She fumbled for her compact, but dropped it back in her purse when Mr. Tomlinson pointed at her.

"Tina," he said, "you're first speaker for the affirmative. Proceed."

Tina nodded and calmly rose to her feet, already composed and confident, the last traces of blush fading from her cheeks.

Nikki had to hand it to her. Tina was a pain, but she could be extremely focused when she needed to be.

"Can we trust our senses?" asked Tina, looking both Mr. Tomlinson and Rufius firmly in the eye. "Of course. Just consider how we see the world. Yes, our brains process the input from our eyes, but the picture produced in our minds is quite similar to what a camera sees and records. There are small deviations from reality, such as the well-known blind spot created by our optic nerves, but our brains compensate for these minor issues and create a reasonable facsimile of the world. The opposing team will try to convince you that your own eyes and ears can't be trusted, but the evidence is clear and reassuring. Your senses aren't playing tricks on you."

Nikki snorted. Tina had noticeably failed to present any 'clear and reassuring' evidence. Other than the comparison of human eyesight to cameras she hadn't presented any evidence at all. Melanie stood up and delivered another evidence-free oration. She was dramatic and memorable, her voice ringing out across the auditorium like a gospel preacher on a roll. Their team was clearly going all out on the emotional comfort approach.

After Melanie Tim delivered what amounted to a sermon extolling the virtues of a mother's touch, which had Mr. Tomlinson giving him a raised eyebrow. He waived Tim back to his seat before the sermon was finished and sighed deeply.

"It seems that some of you have taken my description of the judges a bit too much to heart," said Mr. Tomlinson. "I merely wanted to impress upon you that they aren't experts at rhetoric, not that they're idiots. Even the car dealer is going to be annoyed if you deliver such pablum at the tournament." He gestured at Jamal to stand up. "Let's see if the team arguing the negative can do better."

Jamal spoke carefully and on topic. Nikki thought he struck just the right balance between providing enough evidence to support his points without beating the audience over the head with facts. He was a little robotic, and didn't have Melanie's ability to connect with a crowd, but his centrist approach was a relief after Tim's blatant appeal to emotion.

Allan's attempt to explain the duck versus rabbit illusion was clumsy. For reasons Nikki couldn't understand he decided to drag in Daffy Duck and Bugs Bunny, which drew snickers from the other team. She could only guess that he'd been trying to make his argument more vivid, but Daffy and Bugs refused to slide elegantly into his presentation and instead seemed more like hostages marched in at gunpoint.

When Allan was done Nikki reluctantly rose to her feet. Rufius was staring at her intently, his expression unreadable. She noticed that he had a dark purple bruise on his right temple. She wondered if that was where Bertie had hit him with the rake when they'd fought on the Dinsfeld farm. She tried to follow Tina's example and focus, but she could feel Rufius getting into her head. She shook herself, picked a spot out in the dark auditorium to look at, and began to explain the index of refraction. She was in the middle of Snell's Law when the side door of the auditorium suddenly banged open and someone came charging down the aisle. The stage lights were in her eyes, and she didn't realize it was Bertie until he came to a stop right in front of the stage.

"I need to speak with you immediately," proclaimed Bertie, gesturing wildly for Nikki to come down from the stage.

Mr. Tomlinson's chair scraped loudly across the wooden floor of the stage as he rose to his feet. "Sir, you are interrupting our debate team's practice session. And believe me, they need the practice and cannot afford interruptions. Now, who are you and why are you here? I know you're not a parent, as I've met all the parents of our team members."

"No," said Bertie. "Of course I am not a parent. Never had the slightest inclination for it. Don't have the patience. But I still need to speak to that young lady there." He pointed at Nikki.

"Sir," said Mr. Tomlinson. "I must ask you to leave. If you don't I'll have no choice but to call a security guard."

Rufius rose to his feet, putting a hand on Mr. Tomlinson's shoulder. "Why don't you let me handle this?" he said. "I'll take this gentleman outside and find out what he wants."

"Fine," said Mr. Tomlinson. "Happy to let you deal with it, Radnor." He sat back down in his chair. "Start over from the beginning,

Murrow. And this time leave Snell's Law in your physics textbook where it belongs. The trigonometric calculation of angles does not belong in a debate."

Nikki watched as Rufius sauntered across the stage and down the stairs to where Bertie was standing. He took Bertie by the arm and whispered something in his ear. Whatever it was it seemed to be effective. Bertie slumped and allowed Rufius to lead him out of the auditorium.

Mr. Tomlinson impatiently cleared his throat and Nikki tried to begin again, but her glance kept going to the side door that Rufius and Bertie had disappeared through.

"I'm sorry," she said after starting over three times. "It's just that that man is a family friend and I'm afraid he might be in some kind of trouble. I need to go check." Ignoring the protests of Mr. Tomlinson and Tina she ran down the stage stairs and out the side door. The bright morning sunlight burned her eyes after the darkness of the auditorium and at first she couldn't see where Rufius and Bertie had gone. Finally she spotted them walking across the school's soccer field. As she watched they disappeared into the grove of trees bordering the field.

Nikki broke into a run. She had no idea what she was going to do if she caught up to them, but she couldn't just abandon Bertie. It was clear that Rufius wanted to get him alone in an isolated area.

Her lungs burned as she sprinted across the soccer field and ducked under the low-hanging branches of an oak tree at the edge of the grove. She had to slow her pace as thick, twisted tree roots and piles of rotting leaves made it impossible to run. She picked her way deeper into the trees, listening for voices, but all she could hear was a blue jay squawking somewhere overhead.

The grove wasn't large, not much more than a couple of acres. She walked all the way through the trees and out the other side, emerging onto the hot asphalt of a parking lot baking in the sun. The lot belonged to a Dennys and the morning rush had filled it with cars. Rufius and Bertie were nowhere in sight. She dashed into the restaurant and quickly scanned the booths. Lots of Country Fried Steak and Santa Fe Skillets, but none were being eaten by a couple of escapees from the Realm of Reason. She grabbed a bus boy by the arm and asked if he'd check the men's room for two cousins who she was supposed to meet. He agreed cheerfully enough, but came back shaking his head. Nikki thanked him and hurried out to the parking lot again. Beyond the Dennys stretched miles of residential neighborhoods. She doubted Rufius would lead Bertie in that direction. Too many eyes to spot a couple of men walking down the mostly empty sidewalks. Rufius's electric blue suit was flattering, which was of course why he'd picked it, but it also made him memorable.

Nikki spun on her heel and ran back to the grove of trees. She ducked under the overhanging branches again and started searching. She tried to follow a grid pattern from one side of the grove to the other, but the piles of leaves and small dips and hollows in the bumpy ground made it difficult. When she emerged back onto the soccer field after the last pass through the trees she felt a wave of relief. Bertie was still out and about somewhere in Madison. She'd just decided to head home to enlist the help of Curio in the search, when a man emerged from the trees. He was walking a black lab on a leash and talking on a cell phone.

"Yes," he said into the phone. "That small oak forest behind Westlake High School. I was walking my dog there when I stumbled across him. Well, Soot did, actually. He smelled something and started digging in a pile of leaves. I pulled Soot off of him and checked for a pulse. He's bleeding from a head wound, but he's still breathing. I'm no doctor, but he doesn't look so good. You'd better hurry."

As he put his cell phone in his pocket he noticed Nikki. "You shouldn't stay here, Miss. I'm not sure exactly what happened, but it seems a crime might have been committed. I've called the police and an ambulance." He pointed over at the school parking lot. "There are some other kids over there. Why don't you go join them."

Nikki nodded and headed across the soccer field. She perched on the hood of Tina's red Toyota and waited, trying not to think too hard about what the man's black lab had found. It wasn't long before she heard sirens wailing in the distance.

# Chapter Thirteen

## The Patient

"BERTIE'S *WHERE*?" ASKED Kira.

"In the hospital," said Nikki, sitting down next to Curio on his sleeping-bag bed in the empty apartment. Cation abandoned the can of tuna she'd been picking at and jumped into her lap. "They probably took him to St. Mary's. That's the closest. Anyway, as near as I can guess, Rufius hit him on the head with something after leading him into that small forest near my school. Why Bertie went with him is a mystery. Rufius might have threatened me or Curio, so I guess Bertie felt he needed to protect us. I saw Bertie as he was being loaded into the ambulance. He was conscious. I saw him try to sit up. So that's an encouraging sign."

"But what's a hospital?" asked Kira. "And what's an ambulance?"

"A hospital is a place where they have lots of healers," said Nikki.

Both Kira and Curio winced.

"You mean people like old Fortuna?" asked Curio. "People that sell you smelly potions you can't afford? Potions what burns all the skin clear off yer arm and doesn't fix the problem?"

"No," said Nikki. "Good healers. People who know what they're doing. People like Linnea, the healer from Kingston. She saved a whole bunch of lives during the fighting in ImpHaven, and when Rufius and the Knights of the Iron Fist tried to take over Cogent

Town. She saved Gwen's life. And Krill's."

"Yes, she did," said Kira quietly. "We're both very grateful to her."

"So do we just waits until these healers are done with Mr. Bertie?" asked Curio.

Nikki shook her head. "No, we need to get him out of the hospital as soon as possible. Not if he's seriously injured, of course. But we can't leave him there. You know Bertie. He's going to start talking. He can't help himself. He's going to start telling people he's royalty and that he's from another world. I'm afraid they'll lock him up in the looney bin."

Curio nodded. "I knows what you mean. We had an old tramp in D-ville that used to wander the streets clucking like a chicken. He was harmless as a puppy, but the local shopkeepers didn't like him. He'd carry around an egg and a little wooden stool. He'd pick a shop or a tavern and plop hisself down on that stool right in front of their door. Then he'd tuck the egg under the stool and pretend he was laying it. Most of the locals just laughed at him, especially if they'd been gulping down ale at a tavern. But the shopkeepers got together a petition and sent it to the Mayor of D-ville and he had the old tramp locked up in the City Hall dungeon. Don't know if he ever got out again."

"Exactly," said Nikki. "We can't let something like that happen to Bertie."

"So what are we going to do?" asked Kira.

"I'm not sure," said Nikki, scratching Cation's head. "The first thing to do is confirm which hospital he's in. Madison has several. It'd be easier if I could just call them all, but I don't see how that's going to work. Bertie doesn't have any ID, and I don't think hospitals give out information about crime victims anyway. We'll have to go in person."

"So let's go," said Curio, pulling on his walking boot.

"We need to wait for Krill," said Nikki. "Bertie could be injured and need help walking. He might even need to be carried. Krill is the only one of us who can do that."

"Krill should be back any minute," said Kira. "He said around noon, and it's close to that, judging by the sun."

Nikki nodded. She'd convinced one of the boys in her chemistry class to take Krill to his family's farm. They needed help harvesting two fields of broccoli, and they paid cash. She'd told the boy that Krill was from Botswana, to explain his accent. Madison had a small community of people from Somalia, but immigrants from Botswana seemed rare enough that Krill wasn't likely to encounter any.

Nikki dumped Cation off her lap and stretched out on Curio's sleeping bag, closing her eyes. She needed a plan for Operation Rescue Bertie, but no ideas came to her. The biggest obstacle was that they were all kids. The first thing the hospital staff was going to ask was where their parents were. She sighed. Her year in the Realm of Reason hadn't been easy, but her age had been less of an issue there. Partly because the Realm had medieval safety standards and lots of child labor. Those weren't good things, but the lack of rules sometimes let her get away with things she couldn't here in modern-day Madison Wisconsin.

She was still thinking when the window creaked open and Krill climbed in. He was dusty from head to toe and had bits of broccoli stuck in his hair. He reached into the pocket of his patched suede vest and pulled out a twenty-dollar bill. He handed it to Nikki.

"That's all they gave you?" said Nikki. "For an entire morning's work?"

Krill shrugged. "They also gave us a good breakfast. And something called hamburgers for lunch. They weren't as good as the fried fish back home in Kingston, but they weren't bad. Now if you'll excuse me I need to wash up. Curio, could you help me work the taps? I don't remember which handle I'm supposed to turn."

"Check the stairs first," said Nikki. "And keep the shower as short as possible."

"Of course, Miss," said Curio. He tiptoed to the front door and put his ear to it, listening intently for any sound of someone coming up to the second floor. He gave Krill a thumbs up and herded him into the bathroom like a tiny sheepdog nipping at the heels of a giant sheep.

By the time they returned from the bathroom Nikki had a fuzzy plan in mind. It had some gaping holes in it, but they had to try anyway.

"NOT BAD," SAID Nikki, eyeing Krill up and down.

She, Curio, and Kira were sitting on a bench in front of the emergency department of St. Mary's Hospital. Krill was pacing nervously in front of them.

Krill tugged at the shirt he was wearing. "It's awfully flimsy. I'm used to something sturdier. What kind of cloth is this?"

"Cotton, I think," said Nikki. "Maybe a cotton and nylon blend. They're called scrubs. Goodwill always has a bunch of them for sale. I'm not sure why. Maybe from home healthcare nurses quitting their jobs. I can't say I blame them. It's a rough business."

"What is that stain?" asked Kira, pointing to a faded reddish-brown splotch decorating Krill's left pant leg from knee to ankle.

"Don't think about it," said Nikki. She hadn't had to figure out which hospital Bertie had been taken to after all. The man with the black lab had posted his find on Twitter, and someone from the local news channel had posted that the unknown crime victim had been sent to St. Mary's.

"Okay," she said. "Bertie's mostly likely still in the emergency room. I hope. If they've taken him to the operating room then this isn't going to work. Anyway, emergency rooms can be a little chaotic.

I was in here once when I broke my arm. I crashed my bike on some ice. Ambulances were constantly bringing people in, and nurses were running back and forth and people were yelling. But that's a good thing. It means that Krill should be able to slip in unnoticed.

Krill nodded, anxiously smoothing his dreadlocks. "If anyone asks I say I'm a trainee healer's aid."

"A trainee *nurse's* aid," said Nikki.

"From the nursing program at the school," said Krill.

"From the nursing program at UW," said Nikki.

"Right," said Krill. "UW."

"But try to avoid talking to anyone," said Nikki. "Just walk quickly and pretend you know where you're going. Don't bother with the waiting room. That's the first room you'll see, with lots of people sitting in chairs. Bertie was found unconscious with a head injury. I'm pretty sure they've taken him straight to an exam room. Those are off to the right, just past the waiting room. You'll see a long row of cubicles with curtains in front of them. Check all of them as quickly as you can. If anyone asks what you're doing say you're looking for one of your friends from the nursing program. If you find Bertie you'll have to make a judgment call. If he's unconscious and has tubes and stuff sticking out of him then leave him there and come back here. If he's conscious and recognizes you and starts talking, get him to shut up and see if he can stand. If he can't stand put him in a wheelchair and push him out here."

"Right," said Krill. "And that's a wheelchair." He pointed to an old man who was being wheeled into the emergency room.

"Yes," said Nikki.

"Okay," said Krill, taking a deep breath. "I suddenly wish I was back in the Realm, hauling in a net full of cod. But homesickness will have to wait." He turned on his heel and marched up to the emergency room doors. He jumped when the doors automatically slid open as he approached. He looked back at Nikki in alarm, but she just waved at him to go in. He hurried through, as if expecting the doors to slam shut and slice him in two.

"What makes the doors do that, Miss?" asked Curio. "Is it magic?"

"Of course not," said Nikki. "There's a motion sensor which detects when a person is approaching, and an electric drive train connected to rollers which open and close the doors. Think of the waterwheels you have back in the Realm of Reason. They're a power source, just like an electric motor. And imagine the waterwheel attached to a pulley. If you attached the pulley to a door the force of the water could open it automatically."

Curio listened intently, looking from Nikki to the door. He hopped off the bench and ran up to the door, cautiously tapping the rubber mat in front of the door with one tiny foot. Nothing happened, so he jumped onto the mat with both feet. The door slid open and he darted inside. Five seconds later the door opened again and he was running toward them as fast as he could.

"He's here, Miss!" Curio gasped.

"Who?" asked Nikki.

"Rufius!" said Curio. "He's sitting in a chair, calm as can be."

"Did he see you?" asked Kira.

"No, Miss," said Curio. "His back's to the door."

"What are we going to do?" asked Kira. "Krill's going to bring Bertie right past him."

"We'll have to warn him. Come on," said Nikki. "There's got to be another way inside." She led the way around the side of the building, past the parking lot, to the ambulance bay. An ambulance was just pulling away, its siren shrieking. Two others were parked nearby. The one which had just left had been parked next to a raised platform, where the stretchers could be wheeled inside the hospital without having to lift them down from the vehicle. The door at the end of the platform was still open. Nikki climbed up onto the platform and peeked around the edge of the door. It led to an empty hallway lined with stacks of sheets and towels packaged in plastic.

"Stay here," she whispered to Curio and Kira, who were climbing up onto the platform. "Hide over there," she said, pointing to a cluster of ventilation shafts.

"But Miss," began Curio.

"No time," hissed Nikki. "Hide." She ran down the hall past the stacks of sheets and into the rabbit warren of hallways in the center of the hospital. The yellow signs on the walls and the colorful murals of Winnie the Pooh told her she was in the children's ward. A nurse in purple scrubs was wheeling a young girl on a stretcher straight toward Nikki. The stretcher had a squeaky wheel and the girl was missing her left hand. Nikki tried not to stare. She pretended to be reading a Dr. Seuss poem which was painted on the wall.

"You really shouldn't be here," said the nurse, stopping next to Nikki. "Please go back to the waiting room."

"But," said Nikki, "my parents are with my little sister. Just down there. She's having a procedure and they didn't want me to watch. The waiting room's too far away. I want to be close by." She tried to sound like she'd been crying but it came out more like a frog-croak.

The nurse patted her arm. "All right. Just don't wander into any of the patient rooms."

"No, of course not," said Nikki. "Thank you."

As soon as the stretcher disappeared around a corner Nikki ran in the opposite direction. New signs in green informed her that she had entered the oncology ward. She spotted a map of the hospital on the wall, with a 'You are here' pointer. The emergency room wasn't much farther. Just past oncology and through radiation.

She had to duck into two storage closets and a bathroom to avoid being spotted, but she made it to the emergency ward without being stopped by anyone. This area of the hospital was noisier than oncology. Someone was screaming the name 'Jimmy', and a woman's voice was begging for painkillers. A doctor ran past and disappeared into a cubicle, closing the curtain after him. Nikki slowly inched her way down the long hall of cubicles. There were voices behind the closed curtains but no one directly in sight. That wouldn't last long though, and she had no good reason for being there.

She ducked down and peeked under the nearest curtain. Krill was still wearing his rough sailor's boots under his scrubs. Nope, no luck. The cubicle had a pair of pink Crocs and a pair of day-glo orange ones. The next cubicle had a pair of neon-green Crocs. So did the next. Crocs appeared to be the footwear of choice among medical personnel.

A curtain slid open down at the end of the row of cubicles. Nikki froze. There was no place to hide except for inside one of the cubicles. She was just about to take her chances that the next one was empty when she heard him.

"But I want to go home. *Now.* I miss my feather bed up at the castle. Do you know where I've been sleeping? On the *floor.* People tell me I'm a polite chap, especially for a royal. But my politeness is reaching its limit. I sleep on the floor with a cat jumping on my face half the night. And a little boy bosses me around. Even putting up with Athena is better than this."

Bertie. He sounded about two cubicles down. Nikki ran toward his voice and threw herself down on the floor, peering under the curtain. Krill's boots were nervously tapping on the linoleum. Nikki squirmed under the curtain and put a finger to her lips as a startled Krill stared down at her.

"We need to get him out of here right now," whispered Nikki. "But we can't take him out through the waiting room. Rufius is there."

"Is there a back door?" whispered Krill.

Bertie was lying down on a hospital bed and couldn't see Nikki. "Who are you talking to?" he asked.

Before Krill could answer the curtain was pulled open. Nikki threw herself under the bed just in time.

A pair of pale blue Crocs walked up to the foot of the bed. "Nurse, get a urine sample from this patient," said a woman's voice. "I want to check for drugs. His head wound's not serious, but he's been saying the oddest things."

Krill must have nodded, for the doctor disappeared as quickly as she'd come.

Krill pulled the curtain closed again and crouched down, peering under the bed. "Now what?" he whispered.

"Wheelchair," whispered Nikki.

Krill nodded. "I saw one next door." He disappeared, returning a few seconds later pushing a wheelchair through the curtain.

Nikki crawled out from under the bed.

Bertie shrieked and nearly fell onto the floor. Krill grabbed him and man-handled him into the wheelchair.

"What's happening?" gasped Bertie. "And why does my head hurt?"

"No time," whispered Nikki. She pulled the curtain open and peeked out. Two doctors were arguing about something down at the end of the hall, blocking the way back to the ambulance bay. Nikki led the way in the opposite direction. She walked fast but avoided breaking into a panicked run. They passed an MRI room and a sign for the morgue. Nikki paused, staring at the sign and feeling a bit sick.

"What?" whispered Krill.

"Nothing," said Nikki, breathing a sigh of relief. She'd just spotted a small sign with a red arrow pointing in the direction of the cafeteria. "This way."

No one so much as glanced at them in the crowded cafeteria. Lots of other people were awkwardly negotiating around the Formica-topped tables in wheelchairs and on crutches. Bertie kept trying to climb out of the wheelchair, but Krill put one hand on his shoulder and Nikki helped push the chair. They got him through the cafeteria with only one outburst, when Bertie informed a startled cafeteria worker that he was the King of the Realm of Reason and wanted directions to the nearest portal.

Nikki felt a hysterical need to giggle. She bit her tongue and pushed harder on the wheelchair, shoving Bertie through a side entrance and out into the cold Wisconsin air.

"Do you think you can find your way back home from here?" she asked Krill. "I need to go retrieve Curio and Kira."

"I think so," said Krill.

"If you get lost aim for the lake," said Nikki, pointing at the blue water of Lake Monona sparkling in the sun. "Follow the lakeshore until you get to Bassett Street. You'll see the green and white street sign. Go up Bassett about half a mile and you'll reach my building. Shove Bertie and the wheelchair through the hedge and wait in the side yard. Try to keep him quiet while you're waiting. People can't see through the hedge but they can hear through it."

Krill headed off toward the lake with Bertie complaining loudly about the cold.

Nikki jogged through the hospital parking lot, past the front entrance, and was nearly at the ambulance bay when she rounded a corner and ran smack into Kira.

"Oh thank goodness!," gasped Kira. "I was just about to go inside to look for you. I can't find Curio."

"What!" said Nikki. "Did he go inside?"

"I don't know," said Kira. "We were both hiding, watching that door you disappeared through. Curio was a few feet behind me. After a while I turned to check on him, and he wasn't there. Do you think he went back to your home?"

Nikki shook her head. "No, that doesn't seem like something he'd do. Not without telling us." She looked back at the front entrance to the hospital. "I wonder if he decided to keep an eye on Rufius. That *does* seem like something he'd do. Come on."

They ran to the entrance and through the automatic doors into the waiting room. It was crowded and noisy, with a TV blaring Wheel of Fortune from one corner.

Nikki stood by the door, partially hidden behind a potted Ficus tree, and scanned the room. Curio wasn't there. Neither was Rufius.

"I don't see him," she said to Kira. "Do you?"

"No," said Kira. "Should we try to search the building?"

Nikki reluctantly shook her head. The hospital was huge. If Curio was wandering its halls looking for her it would be almost impossible to find him. Not without being noticed by hospital personnel and ordered back to the waiting room. She hesitated, uncertain what to do. There weren't any good options.

"We'll wait," she finally said. "You stay here and I'll go back to the ambulance bay where you were hiding. If Curio's still in the hospital he'll eventually come back here or to the ambulance bay to find us."

"No," said Kira. "It's too dangerous for you. I'm not sure if Rufius remembers me. He only saw me at that card game in the Count of Calumnia's tower. I was disguised as a parlor maid and had a cap covering my braids. But you're a different story. Rufius definitely knows *you.* If he's still hanging around he might spot you. It's too isolated out there. There'd be no one to help if he came after you."

Nikki yanked at her hair in frustration. She knew Kira was right, but she couldn't go back home without Curio. "Krill," she finally said. "He stands a better chance against Rufius. We'll have him watch the ambulance bay. He can't be far. It's slow work pushing Bertie in that wheelchair. I sent them back to my house, but they can't be more than a few blocks away yet. Come on."

She led Kira to the side of the hospital facing the lake. The building was on a small hill and they could see the lakeshore and its neighboring residential areas all the way to the white dome of the state capital building in the distance.

"There," said Nikki, pointing. "That's them. They're just passing that Chinese restaurant. See that red building with the gold letters and the hanging lanterns?"

Kira nodded. "But what's the plan? Krill and I bring Bertie back here?"

"No," said Nikki. "Send Krill back here and you push Bertie to my house. Or get him to walk if he can. You should be safer down there than up here. And try to keep Bertie quiet, especially once you get him into my side yard. He's a handful at the best of times, and he'll be even worse with a head injury, but it's important that my Mom and our downstairs neighbor don't find out that all of you are staying in the empty apartment. The last thing we need is the police arresting all of you for squatting."

"What's squatting?" asked Kira.

"Never mind," said Nikki. "Just run after them before they get too far ahead. I'll go back and sit in the waiting room." She watched Kira until she disappeared behind a parked delivery van. Nikki walked back to the waiting room and sat in the back row of chairs next to a construction worker with a bloody bandage on his arm.

"Drilled myself," said the construction worker, holding up his arm. Drops of blood fell onto his neon-yellow vest. "My hands were sweaty. Should have been wearing gloves, but I was in a hurry to get done for the day. My hand slipped and the drill bit went right into my arm."

"I'm sorry," said Nikki, looking at him in alarm. "Shouldn't you be up there in front instead of way back here?"

"Nah," said the construction worker. "There's more serious cases ahead of me. The drill didn't go in too deep. It looks worse than it is cause of all the blood."

"Okay, if you say so," said Nikki, looking unconvinced. "I hate to bother you, but have you seen a guy in an electric blue suit? He's really pale, with black hair."

"Oh sure," said the construction worker. "Noticed him right away. Weird looking dude. Looked like he was auditioning for a movie about the Rolling Stones. Looked a bit like Keith Richards in his younger days."

Nikki nodded. "Yes, that's him. Did you see where he went?"

"Sure," said the construction worker. "He went out that way about twenty minutes ago." He pointed to the entrance doors.

"Thanks," said Nikki, jumping up.

"Hey," shouted the construction worker as she hurried to the entrance. "The guy looked like bad news. You shouldn't be hanging around with him."

Nikki just waved at him as she ran through the automatic doors. The sun was starting to set and she shivered in the cold evening air as she tried to decide what to do. If Curio had spotted Rufius leaving and followed him things might have gone very bad very quickly. She tried to think where Rufius might go. This late in the day on a Saturday it was unlikely that he would go back to her high school. The debate team practice was long over. He might go into a bar, but it seemed unlikely. Back in the Realm he'd never been much of a drinker. He was far more inclined to get other people drunk so that he could manipulate them. She looked off in the distance toward the state capital building. The YMCA was only a few blocks away from it. As far as she knew Rufius was still living there. She zipped up her jacket and headed in that direction.

# Chapter Fourteen

## Missing

"WE SHOULD BE out looking for him," said Kira, her braids swinging as she paced back and forth in the empty apartment.

"I know," said Nikki. "But we need a place to start. We can't search all of Madison."

"Perhaps they've gone back through the portal," said Bertie. He was tucked into his sleeping bag on the floor. Cation was sniffing at the bandages on his head. "Maybe Rufius thought that little Curio could open it for him."

Nikki shook her head. "No, Rufius already knows that Curio can't open the portal."

"You're sure that Rufius doesn't have Curio locked up in his room?" asked Krill. "In that place. What was its name again?"

"The Y," said Nikki. "And yes, I'm sure. I convinced the front desk clerk to let me have a quick look in Rufius's room. I said my little brother was missing. No one was there. I checked under the bed and in the closet. There was nothing in the closet but Rufius's purple suit."

"Maybe little Curio sprouted wings and is flying above the treetops," said Bertie.

Nikki, Kira, and Krill all stared at him.

"Maybe we shouldn't have taken him out of that building full of healers," said Krill. "He doesn't seem quite right in the head. Do you want me to wheel him back there?"

"No," said Nikki. "We'll just have to keep a close eye on him. If he starts to get worse we'll take him to the local emergency clinic. It's closer than the hospital."

"The first time I had a fencing lesson I stabbed myself in the big toe," Bertie announced, giving Cation a scritch under the chin. She was perched on his chest, licking at a deep scratch on his cheek. "All male nobles in the Realm have to learn sword fighting. I had my first lesson at thirteen. After the toe incident I had the royal shoemaker add extra layers of leather to the tops of all my boots. I was also required to learn fisticuffs. The first time I managed to land a blow on my opponent I broke two fingers."

"That's nice," said Kira, tucking Bertie's sleeping bag up to his chin. "Why don't you try to have a little nap?"

"No, you miss my point," said Bertie. "What I mean to say is that as a royal and a noble I learned the arts of swordplay and fisticuffs from a young age. Rufius did not. He was a cheesemonger's son. Of low birth. People of his class do not grow up learning the martial arts. This deficiency was very apparent when he attacked me in the forest. He swung wildly and without much effect. I was getting the better of him when I tripped and fell over a log. He grabbed a fallen branch and hit me several times on the head. I suppose I must have blacked out. My main point is that no, contrary to what you may think, I am not a rare spotted bullfrog, and that my injuries could have been much worse if Rufius knew what he was doing."

"Bullfrog?" said Krill, grinning.

Nikki shrugged. "He seems to be partly making sense and partly spinning fantasies. I guess it's the head injury. Or maybe they gave him some drugs in the hospital. If he's still saying weird stuff by tomorrow morning we'll take him to the local clinic."

A soft rattling sound suddenly came from the bedroom window.

Nikki ran to it and threw open the sash.

"Just a squirrel," she said bitterly, closing the window again.

"Maybe Curio's just lost," said Kira, giving Nikki's arm a reassuring pat.

Nikki shook her head. "No. He's been here for more than a week now. He knows the local area really well. This neighborhood, the lake, my school. He's not lost. Rufius has him. I'm sure of it."

"You're probably right," said Krill, sitting down on the floor and stretching his long legs in front of him. "But the question is, what does Rufius want with him? He already knows that Curio can't open the portal. Does he plan to use him as a hostage? To force *you* to open the portal?"

"No," said Nikki. "He knows I can't open the portal either."

"Maybe Rufius is going to ask us for a ransom," said Kira. "Does he need money?"

"Not as much as he did when he first arrived here," said Nikki. "He managed to swindle his way into a decent-paying job at my school. He even convinced them to pay him in cash. I heard the assistant principal talking about it in the hall. He was laughing at Rufius for being a foreigner and not even knowing how a checking account worked. It's unusual to get paid in cash here. Most people have bank accounts. But of course Rufius wouldn't know how those work. Anyway, he's not rolling in money but he's got enough to live on."

"That's not enough," said Bertie, trying to sit up.

Kira gently pushed him back down.

"Rufius requires mountains of money," said Bertie. "Rivers of gold coins. Fountains of silver. He's the greediest person I've ever met, and I've met many a noble who'd sell his own grandmother for a bag of gold. Of course, the greediest creatures in the Realm are the blue jays. They steal gold every chance they get. You should see the hoards of gold coins they have stashed in pine trees all over the Realm."

"Leaving aside the blue jays," said Krill. "I don't really see how asking us for a ransom is a smart thing to do. None of us have any money."

"That's not quite true," said Nikki. "There's Bertie's bag of gold coins that he brought with him when he came through the portal. I buried it out in the side yard, under the hedge."

"Does Rufius know about it?" asked Kira.

Nikki shook her head. "No, I don't think so." She looked at Bertie. "You didn't tell Rufius about your gold, did you?"

Bertie snorted. "Of course not madame. I may not be the smartest person in the Realm, but I have more sense than that. Rufius would cut my throat for just one gold coin, much less a whole bag full. But I did tell Robin about it. He was flitting around the ivy outside, pecking at a worm crawling up the brick wall of your house. He seemed like he could keep a secret, so I told him about the gold. But don't worry, robins are the most trustworthy of birds, unlike blue jays."

Nikki ignored this. She'd just had an idea. "Fortuna," she exclaimed. "If Rufius has Curio he needs a place to stash him, and Fortuna's psychic shop might be just the place. She said the owner of the shop gave her a little room at the back of the shop to sleep in."

"Fortuna the Fortunate's here?" asked Kira. "Good gravy, how many of the Realm's citizens have come here?"

"Just Curio, Rufius, Fortuna, Bertie, and you two," said Nikki. "Oh, and one sheep. It's wandering around near my school somewhere. Kira, stay here and keep an eye on Bertie. Me and Krill will go check out Fortuna's shop."

Night had fallen. Nikki opened the bedroom window and climbed down through the ivy in the dark. She squirmed under the hedge and looked up and down the street. The sidewalks were empty. "This way," she whispered to Krill as he emerged from the gap under the hedge. She walked fast, heading toward the lights of downtown. Their glow seemed to promise success and safety. They'd find Curio and he'd be safe and sound.

Nikki muttered 'safe and sound' under her breath as she walked even faster.

End of *The Trouble With Portals*

Nikki's adventures continue in Book Two of the series
Logic to the Rescue 2

**The Logic to the Rescue series**

*Logic to the Rescue*
*The Prince of Physics*
*The Bard of Biology*
*Mystics and Medicine*
*The Sorcerer of the Stars*
*Warlock of the Wind*
*The Engineer of Evil*
*Math and Manners*

**The Logic to the Rescue 2 series**

*The Trouble with Portals*

**The Hamsters Rule series**

*Hamsters Rule, Gerbils Drool*
*Hamsters Rule the School*

**Mystery Novels**

*The Gostynin Shul*
*The Danger Next Door*
*The Danger Down Under*

www.ingramcontent.com/pod-product-compliance
Lightning Source LLC
LaVergne TN
LVHW010607160826
845677LV00013B/3289

* 9 7 9 8 8 6 9 0 8 1 4 6 9 *